ITALIAN DEVIL'S BABY

HEIDI RICE

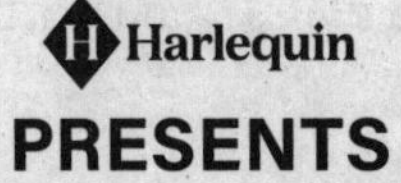

Harlequin

PRESENTS

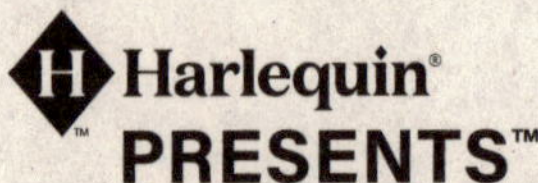

Harlequin®
PRESENTS™

Recycling programs for this product may not exist in your area.

ISBN-13: 978-1-335-21391-4

Italian Devil's Baby

Harlequin Enterprises ULC
22 Adelaide St. West, 41st Floor
Toronto, Ontario M5H 4E3, Canada
www.Harlequin.com

HarperCollins Publishers
Macken House, 39/40 Mayor Street Upper,
Dublin 1, D01 C9W8, Ireland
www.HarperCollins.com

Printed in Lithuania

1 2 3 4 5 6 7 8 9 10 LIT 28 27 26 25

"Vito?" I whispered, sure I had to be hallucinating.

Clearly the pregnancy hormones weren't through messing with me just yet. But then he spoke again, his voice hoarse with accusation, and the shock constricted around my throat.

"Il bambino é mio, si." The sharp words sliced through what was left of my composure, as his penetrating gaze rose back to my face—the searing accusation in his eyes burning my skin.

My shattered mind started to engage.

Of course, he could have gotten in here, Mia. The guy's a bloody mafia don, you melt.

I didn't speak Italian, but it wasn't hard to guess what he had asked me. The lie hovered on my tongue. If I told him the baby wasn't his, would this vision disappear?

Did I want it to disappear?

And reality returned in a rush.

This was real. Vito was here, in my home. And now he knew about the baby.

A steamy new duet from
USA TODAY bestselling author Heidi Rice!

Captive Mafia Seductions

Their world is dark, dangerous and deeply tempting…

Vittorio, southern Italy's most feared mafia boss, is in a violent play for power with his half brother Dante. They both crave the same goal—supremacy of the Rocco syndicate. Not even the law could hold them back. Their only complication? The innocent sisters getting caught in the crossfire!

All her life, Mia has played by the rules. Until lethally attractive Vito captures her eye. He's merciless. She should run. Instead, he shows her how intoxicating recklessness can be. But falling for the mafia king comes with an earth-shattering, nine-month consequence…

Discover Vito and Mia's story in

Italian Devil's Baby

Available now!

And check out Dante and Evie's story

Coming soon!

USA TODAY bestselling author **Heidi Rice** lives in London, England. She is married with two teenage sons—which gives her rather too much of an insight into the male psyche—and also works as a film journalist. She adores her job, which involves getting swept up in a world of high emotions; sensual excitement; funny, feisty women; sexy, tortured men; and glamorous locations where laundry doesn't exist. Once she turns off her computer, she often does chores—usually involving laundry!

Books by Heidi Rice

Harlequin Presents

Hidden Heir with His Housekeeper
Revenge in Paradise
Billionaire's Wedlocked Wife

Billion-Dollar Bet

After-Party Consequences

By Royal Arrangement

Queen's Winter Wedding Charade
Princess for the Headlines

Claimed by a Greek

The Heir Affair
Greek's Kidnapped Princess

Enemy Tycoons

Boss's Bride Price

Visit the Author Profile page
at Harlequin.com for more titles.

To Rob, my Italian connection xx

CHAPTER ONE

Mia

'MIA, ONE OF Vittorio Rocco's security guys is coming our way…and he's looking directly at you.'

When my kid sister Evie whisper-shouted that in my ear, the neglected spot in my panties throbbed in time with the dance music and the strobe lighting and my palpitating heartbeat on the superyacht we'd boarded two hours ago. The superyacht owned by Rocco, which had looked more like a small cruise ship when we'd arrived at the dock in Naples with Evie's best friends, Jessie and Becca.

After two days in the city, doing all the touristy things we could fit in around eating as much pizza as was humanly possible, the four of us had spent all day today shopping for the perfect frock, then getting mani-pedis and our hair done at a tiny salon near our budget hotel. But nothing could have prepared me for an event, or a location, this glamorous and exclusive.

This was the first foreign holiday Evie and I had ever been able to afford. I'd maxed out my credit card buying our dresses this afternoon at a boutique on the Via Toledo. Evie and I had been surviving on our own since we were teenagers, and our mum had skipped out on us, so this wasn't a regular experience.

We'd rubbed shoulders for two hours—like, *literally*—with a string of European celebrities, A-list film stars, supermodels and social media influencers, and those were just the people I recognised. But I still felt as if I were floating in a weird alternative reality—an exhilarating, breathtaking dream which made me feel like a total imposter.

'Oh. My. God! Mia, Evie's not wrong. He must be coming to get you for his boss after "the look",' Becca supplied with additional air quotes. Becca was the one who had somehow finagled an invite to this event for us all through her work. 'We should make ourselves scarce, so he knows you're available.'

'Don't you dare disappear!' I whisper-shouted back while grabbing Evie's arm to keep my sister by my side.

The sultry spring evening scented with sea salt and expensive perfume was almost as breathtaking as the spectacular view across the bay, gilded by moonlight, from the open deck of the yacht, where a world-famous DJ was performing.

Nothing, though, had been as breathtaking as the man I'd first seen standing alone on the top deck of the yacht while we were having our IDs checked and photographed by the phalanx of security personnel before being allowed on board.

We'd figured out from the whispers in the line of guests the man was our host, Vittorio Rocco. Becca, who worked for a brand marketing consortium in the City of London—hence the invite—said no one knew much about him, except that he was an immensely rich local businessman.

But then, twenty minutes ago, he'd strode through the crowd with a couple of bodyguards—greeting a few of the guests but ignoring the rest—before I got 'the look' I was still struggling to decipher. Was he into me, or was he aware I was a total imposter?

As he passed our group, his gaze had locked on mine for what felt like an eternity… Good thing it wasn't an eternity, because I had stopped breathing, my heart slowing to pound between my thighs.

Up close, he was the hottest man I'd ever seen… His gaze was like a heat-seeking missile, scorching everything it touched.

At six-foot-three or-four, with a cut body perfectly displayed in an expertly tailored designer suit, and the sort of tanned, chiselled features which wouldn't look out of place on a catwalk, he had literally oozed sex and dominance. After that heart-stopping eye clash, the four of us had been dissecting and analysing 'the look' in exhaustive detail while the DJ kicked off his set…

But—even though I was wearing my first thong, a mini-dress I'd spent a month's salary on, a push-up bra which made my boobs look like a work of art and killer heels I could barely walk in—I had never expected 'the look' to lead to anything.

Why would this man notice me when there were so many other, more stunning and sophisticated women here?

Supposedly, I was here to cut loose, live a little after spending the last seven years being a stand-in mum to Evie, and finally shake off the shackles of a three-year relationship which had ended in humiliation and heartbreak six months ago…and hopefully finally get laid by someone who knew where a clitoris was, so I could forget about my cheating ex-fiancé Dave and our vanilla sex life.

Or rather, that's what Evie had talked me into when we'd agreed to come on this girl trip together with her friends and make the most of Becca's invite.

But what if 'the look' *had* been real—and not just something we'd embellished with our fertile imaginations? What if the billionaire owner of this superyacht had *really* been checking me out?

Evie was the hopeless romantic. Not me.

I sucked in several deep breaths to build up the courage to glance over my shoulder.

'Is he still headed our way?' I whispered to Evie.

'Yes,' she hissed back. 'And it's definitely you he's headed for. He *has* to be here on Rocco's orders. We *told* you he was checking you out. You look spectacular in that dress, Mia. Why are you even surprised?'

A bubble of laughter eased past the tightness in my ribs.

Evie had been trying to rebuild my confidence ever since I'd kicked Dave to the curb, so she was definitely exaggerating.

In a super casual move, I swept my hair behind my ear and inched my head around.

Then all the air sucked out of my lungs. Because one of the bodyguards Rocco had walked through the crowd with earlier was standing right in front of me, wearing a sharp suit and a frown.

'Will you come upstairs with me, Signorina Taylor. Signor Rocco would like to meet you,' the man said in heavily accented English.

I blinked, feeling light-headed. Was this actually happening? Had my vanilla life finally located some much-needed spice? Or was this all just an illusion caused by oxygen deprivation?

Then Evie woke me up by squealing right in my ear. 'He *was* checking you out. I told you so. The dress totally worked.'

'Umm,' I replied, trembling now with a mix of exhilaration and panic, still struggling to breathe and wanting to kick Evie, because—subtle much, little sis? 'That… Okay, if you're sure it's me he wants to see.'

'*Si*, it is you,' the messenger replied, then held out his arm, directing me towards the spiral staircase which led up to the top deck where his boss had disappeared ten minutes ago. 'Follow me, *per favore*.'

I grasped Evie's hand, intimidated now as well as dazed. 'Can I bring my sister?'

He glanced at Evie, but before he could make a decision, Evie said, 'Rocco doesn't want to see me.'

'No way am I going up there on my own. This was your idea,' I murmured as I tightened my grip on Evie's hand.

But then the bodyguard spoke. 'Don Vito has not asked to see her, only you.'

Evie eased her hand out of my grasp. 'You don't need me with you, Mia. This is your moment. Enjoy it.'

Then Becca weighed in. 'Don't overthink this, Mia. You should totally go for it.'

'But…'

'No buts, Mia. We'll be here waiting to hear all the dirty deets when you get back.' Jessie grinned while wriggling her eyebrows at me.

I breathed out a heavy sigh.

'Don Vito does not like to be kept waiting,' the bodyguard said impatiently.

Don Vito sounded super arrogant, I decided. But even

so, I forced myself to turn to the guard and nod. 'Okay, I'm coming.'

After all, the guy was our host, and he was the hottest man I'd ever seen. So, there was that.

Becca and Jessie and Evie were hooting in triumph and toasting me with their champagne flutes as I followed the guard, which would have been embarrassing in front of this crowd of uber-sophisticated people, but I was too busy struggling to breathe and not trip over my killer heels.

He led me up a spiral staircase behind the DJ booth, to the top deck, where a small group of men in suits was gathered around an opulent bar area. Some of them appeared to be bodyguards. I could see wires coming from their earpieces.

The view of the bay was even more spectacular from this level, the lights of Naples sprinkled over the hills in the distance, while Capri and the Amalfi Coast sparkled like diamonds in the darkness. Inquisitive stares followed us as the guard and I walked past the bar and along a walkway to an isolated area at the back of the yacht, cut off from the rest of the party. A floodlit hot tub stood at the far end—steam rising from the open top—but there was no one in it.

Vittorio Rocco sat alone on one of the leather bench seats which circled the deck, tapping out something on his phone, but as soon as I stepped into the space, he put the phone down and watched me approach. My breath clogged in my lungs, but having his eyes on me added a seductive sway to my hips they'd never had before…or maybe it was just the heels, which required a balancing act to walk in I must have finally mastered.

Too soon I found myself in front of him. He made no

move to get up. Instead, he inclined his head towards the bodyguard. '*Vai via,* Lorenzo.'

'*Si, padrone,*' the man replied. And suddenly we were alone on the secluded deck.

A soft breeze brushed my nape, making the tendrils hanging from my chignon dance across my neck. I shivered, but I wasn't cold.

Even from his position on the couch, our host looked overwhelming—sleek, muscular and devastating. He'd lost the suit jacket and wore a pec-hugging black T-shirt, making the array of tattoos on his arms and around his neck visible. With his face lit by the lights from the yacht's wheelhouse above us, I could also see a couple of scars, one cutting into the stubble on his chin, the other slicing through his eyebrow. The silver cross he wore around his neck seemed incongruous, because he looked like a panther…an extremely hot panther, ready to pounce.

The intense cerulean blue of his irises glittered as he dipped his head to do a roll-call of my entire body.

'*Ciao,* Mia,' he murmured. That he knew my name didn't really surprise me. After all, the guard had addressed me personally downstairs. But on his lips, it sounded impossibly intimate.

'Hello, Mr Rocco,' I replied, deciding I probably shouldn't address him as Vittorio if I didn't want to start hyperventilating.

Maybe this was too much excitement for a teaching assistant from West London, because I was becoming light-headed.

He tilted his head to one side. 'How do you know my name?' he asked, confusing me even more.

'S-some of the other guests mentioned it,' I murmured. I knew his name hadn't been on the invitation, because even Becca hadn't known who was throwing the party until we'd arrived. But was his identity supposed to be a secret?

'And how did you get an invitation to this event?' he asked, his gruff tone cutting through the hum of sound from the DJ set below us…and my chaotic heartbeat.

The question threw me again. Probably because I was still struggling to draw air into my lungs. But then the significance of it hit me…and what that 'look' had really been about. My chaotic heartbeat sank into my killer heels, humiliation washing over me.

He had spotted me in the crowd and realised I didn't belong.

'B-becca. I—I mean Rebecca…' I hesitated, racking my brains to recall Becca's surname, even though I'd known her and Jessie since Evie was in primary school. 'Garner.' *Thank god.* 'My friend Rebecca Garner got an invite. She's here representing her brand marketing firm in London.' Whose company name I could not have remembered right now if he paid me a billion quid.

One eyebrow arched. Then he leaned forward and placed his forearms on his knees, making his biceps and triceps bulge distractingly under his T-shirt. 'And who are *you* here representing, Mia?'

The heat in my thong surged into my cheeks. And the humiliation which had been incinerated with everything else at the sight of those inked forearms came surging back.

'My-myself,' I said, because there was no point in pretending I knew anything about brand marketing. Or that I really had any right to be at his very exclusive party.

His lips quirked. 'I see,' he said, but I couldn't tell whether he was amused or astonished by my gall.

I forced myself to maintain eye contact even though I was dying inside.

Was he about to kick me off the yacht?

I was crestfallen but also determined not to show it as my silly hopes and dreams for the night crashed and burned into a bonfire of embarrassment under that inscrutable gaze.

'And what of the other women with you?' he asked.

'One of them is my sister Evie, the other a friend of ours,' I murmured.

God, he *was* going to kick us all out. While I was resigned to leaving myself, I felt sick for Evie and Jessie, who were having so much fun…and Becca. What if she lost her job? For bringing us along on her invite? From what she'd told us, this man was extremely powerful.

'It's okay, Mr Rocco. We'll leave,' I said, suddenly desperate to get us all out of here before this got any worse.

I turned, keen to get off the yacht. But before I could take a single step, a strong hand captured my wrist.

I swung back round, and my nose connected with a slab of muscle covered in black cotton. Rocco was no longer sitting on the couch but standing close enough to make the air back up in my lungs.

The panther has pounced.

He touched a knuckle under my chin to lift my gaze to his, then leaned in. I sucked in a lungful of his intoxicating scent—woodsy cologne, clean laundry detergent and a hint of orange from the negroni he must have been drinking.

'And how will you leave, Mia?' he whispered, so close to my ear lobe that sensation streaked down my spine and turned my thong into a vibrator. 'Will you swim back to Naples?'

I drew my head back and saw his amusement at my expense. Had he been baiting me all along? That he had humiliated me intentionally had irritation replacing my embarrassment.

'If I have to, yes!' I announced, tugging my wrist free of his grasp. 'I won't stay where I'm not wanted. And I'm not here to be the butt of your jokes.'

Something flashed in his eyes which looked like admiration. 'Who said you are not wanted here, Mia?' he murmured.

My indignation increased at the mocking tone, even as the throbbing in my panties became catastrophic from the sparkle of approval in his gaze. 'You did…or you implied it.'

He chuckled, the sound full of masculine arrogance. 'You have spirit. I like this in a woman.'

Heat swelled in my abdomen. Embarrassing me. How could I be turned on—when he was making fun of me?

He murmured, 'You are also *molto bella*, Mia.' The compliment came so far out of left field, it stunned me into silence. 'I like this, too, in a woman.'

'If you like me so much, why did you ask me to leave?' I managed, even as I could feel my resistance losing ground fast.

His scarred eyebrow quirked, but the sensual smile oozed confidence. 'This I did not do, Mia, when I want to touch you very much.'

My indignation dissolved in a heartbeat as I stood under that startlingly intense gaze, mesmerised by his compliment. And the glitter of approval in his eyes. The surge of validation—that feeling of being seen and wanted by this man, the way I'd never really been wanted by

Dave—was so intoxicating, I felt as if I had just chugged five tequila slammers in a row.

'Do you want to be touched, Mia?' The question was delivered with mocking arrogance, because he already knew the answer.

But even so, I couldn't prevent myself from giving him the permission he sought as my answer popped out in a heady rush of breath. 'Y-yes...'

His smile turned feral, but it only made him look hotter as he lifted his hand to glide his thumb over the thundering pulse in my neck.

I gasped and trembled, his touch like a lightning rod to senses too long denied.

'*Brava ragazza,*' he murmured as he caressed my collarbone—watching my reaction, intently—then slid his thumb under the strap of my mini-dress. My nipples swelled into tight peaks, and I sucked in a shallow breath, already yearning for him to move his roaming thumb lower, the shockingly possessive touch intoxicating.

'I am returning to my estate in Naples. Would you like to come with me for tonight?'

Wh-what?

Was he saying what I thought he was saying? And how did I feel about it? Shouldn't I be insulted? He'd made me feel like nothing a moment ago.

But the truth was, I was too shocked by his bold invitation and my live wire reaction to his touch to focus.

I blinked, stalling for time, until I could regain the power of speech—and critical thinking. Not easy when the hottest guy I had ever laid eyes on had just propositioned me. My usual caution was struggling to play catch up with my over-stimulated libido.

This wasn't me... I'd never been reckless. I didn't like

anything to be out of my control. I was a micro-manager, a planner, a plotter, an over-thinker, someone who always had to be sure of her next move before taking it. All thanks to my mum—a nineties wild child with daughters by two different deadbeats—whose philosophy of life had been, 'Everything will work out in the end if you don't take responsibility for anything.'

Newsflash: It won't.

If you don't pay your rent, the bailiffs will turn up at your door. And you and your daughters will end up climbing out the window in the middle of the night.

I had never wanted to return to the endless chaos of my and Evie's childhood, but this trip…and the Dave debacle…had forced me to realise I might have over-compensated.

Because hadn't my play-it-safe strategy led to a long, boring relationship with the first boy to ever ask me out? And all my over-planning and never making a move before I was one hundred percent sure of a positive outcome had not prevented me ending up engaged to a man who had not only turned out to be a rat but had never come close to satisfying me in bed.

Sometimes life threw you curveballs, which you couldn't plan your way out of.

Evie was right. It was time I kicked myself out of my comfort zone. Time to take a risk and have the wild night I had been aiming for when I'd agreed to come on this trip and spent a fortune on this dress, so my life never got so boring again. Then maybe I'd be better prepared for the next curveball.

I was just debating, though, whether it would be fair to jettison Evie and her friends for the evening, when he placed his hand on my hip and drew me close enough to press my breasts against his chest. My nipples hardened even more and my frantic heartbeat slowed to throb painfully between my thighs as he clasped my neck and pressed his forehead to mine.

'You are fierce, Mia,' he said. 'Taming you will make this night all the sweeter. But first I must kiss you.'

Heat charged through my body. His confidence as hot as his demand.

The fact he had found my attitude a turn-on was addictive—and surprisingly validating.

I'd never been able to let my badass side loose before, but it had always been there, seething beneath the surface, every time my mum made another selfish decision, or Evie did something reckless, or Dave left me unsatisfied…

'You are the most arrogant man on the planet,' I murmured.

He let out another gruff chuckle. '*Si, naturalmente,*' he announced without an ounce of shame.

Then, without waiting for an invitation, he slanted his lips across mine—taking my mouth in a demanding kiss as if it were his right. His lips were firm and warm, his tongue coaxing but insistent. I opened for him instinctively, and he thrust deep as his other hand slid under the hem of my mini-dress.

I gasped, clinging to him now, my whole body vibrating with want, the desire to feel his hands on me as intoxicating as his kiss.

He explored the naked flesh with scalding entitlement, his thumb hooking under the string of my thong. He gave it a sharp tug, rubbing the lace against my aching clitoris. I rose on tiptoe, desperate to ease the pressure, even as his tongue continued to command my mouth, demanding my surrender.

I was panting, groaning, already close to orgasm and struggling to control the sensations powering through my body when he dragged his mouth away abruptly.

I stood gasping for more, caught between the need to come and the need to exert control over what was happening, too fast. I grasped his forearms to steady myself. The inked flesh bunched beneath my fingers, the surprise at how quickly he had got me worked up almost as shocking as the raw ache in my sex still tormenting me.

He released the thong string with a sharp snap, then tugged down the hem of my dress.

'Now you must tell me, Mia,' he said, his tone raw as he continued to caress my shoulders. 'Yes, or no?'

I swallowed, not quite able to speak, the shock of sensations he had conjured and controlled so effortlessly still playing havoc with my common sense.

But while I couldn't resist leaning into his touch, I couldn't banish my usual caution completely. Maybe it was the tats, or the scars, or just the aura of power and wealth which clung to him, and which I had never encountered before…but I didn't want to throw myself into the arms of an *actual* panther.

'How do I know I'll be safe with you?' I asked.

His eyes flashed with something fierce, his scarred eyebrow lifting. Then he laughed. The deep, appreciative rumble reverberated in my abdomen.

'*Safe?*' He let out another rusty chuckle. 'If you want safe, I am the wrong man.'

Why did that sound like a promise rather than a problem?

His caressing hand slid over my shoulder and trailed

down my spine to flatten against the small of my back, setting off a firework display en route. Then my belly connected with the prominent ridge in his trousers.

He brushed his lips across my ear, giving me another intoxicating lungful of pine and orange and laundry soap.

'But you will not be hurt…' he murmured. 'You have my word.' The gravitas in his tone was contradicted by the feral heat in his eyes as his gaze met mine—and the liberties he had already taken—but I believed him.

Then it occurred to me that I wasn't sure I wanted to be safe tonight.

'What about my sister and her friends?' I asked, not quite able to let go of the responsibility that had defined my life for so long. 'I should let Evie know where I'm going…'

He nodded. 'Of course.' His lips quirked in another dangerous smile. 'As long as you do not take too long.'

I let out a breathless laugh. My mind—or rather, what was left of it after that incredible kiss—was made up.

Tonight, I wanted to be wild. And free. And listen to my instincts instead of my insecurities. Because my body was telling me—no, *screaming* at me—that however dangerous this man was, this could be the most exciting night of my life.

'Okay, then, I'd like to accept your invitation,' I said.

CHAPTER TWO

Mia

I WAS STILL struggling not to hyperventilate five minutes later, after saying goodbye to Evie and her friends and collecting my clutch bag from them, when Vito folded his large hand around my trembling fingers and led me to the lower deck.

A gleaming black speedboat was moored to a platform at the back of the superyacht, its engine purring. A driver wearing a peaked cap and uniform shirt stood at the helm, while another collection of Vito's ubiquitous bodyguards waited for us to board.

Vito stepped onto the gently swaying boat, then held out his hand. I hesitated, concerned about the heels.

Before I could overthink it, I kicked them off, picked them up, then took his hand to hop onto the boat.

He chuckled, his eyes alight with amusement, before taking the shoes and my purse to hand to the bodyguard who had followed us onto the boat.

'I didn't want to fall on my bum,' I said by way of explanation.

'You are unconventional, Mia. I like this also,' he said, making me stupidly happy when he laughed again.

I had no idea why, but I had the strangest feeling he didn't laugh very often.

'And it would be a shame for you to fall on your bum,' he said, mimicking my London accent as his strong, callused fingers wrapped around my palm and he led me to the seat just behind the driver. His gaze roamed down, making me aware of the sea breeze on my bare legs. 'When you have such a perfect one.'

'True,' I said, feeling bold and beautiful when he chuckled again.

The bodyguard untied the guide rope as we settled on the seat together.

Suddenly we were speeding across the bay, the pounding bass beat from the DJ set fading. Vito's arm stretched casually across the seat behind me, cocooning me from the misty spray with his strong body. I was pressed back into the seat as the powerful boat lifted into the surf and we charged across the dark water towards Naples.

My heartbeat continued to pummel my ribs, my insane bravado making me almost as dizzy as my first speedboat ride.

Conversation was impossible above the noise of the engine and the shallow waves whipping against the boat's hull. But it seemed to take only seconds to arrive at the private dock where we had boarded the yacht earlier in the evening.

Vito took my hand again to help me out of the boat. He spoke briefly to a couple more bodyguards waiting on the quay, and the guard on the boat handed me back my shoes. I slipped on the high heels. Then Vito grasped my hand again to lead me up the wooden walkway, followed by the security detail.

'You have a lot of bodyguards,' I said.

He glanced at me, surprise flickering in his eyes before he replied. 'It is necessary for our protection.'

Protection from what? I wondered, but the thought got lost when we reached the dock's main concourse, and I spotted an enormous black helicopter—its blades already rotating.

When Vito headed towards it, my hand still gripped in his, I found myself pulling back. He turned to stare at me inquisitively.

'Where is your estate?' I asked, starting to feel overwhelmed.

'In the hills above the city,' he said, but then, probably sensing my panic, he lifted my hand to his lips and brushed a kiss across the knuckles. The gallant gesture was belied by the hot look in his eyes. 'You are afraid to fly?'

'No… It's just… I've never flown in a helicopter before,' I said, trying to swallow the lump of overwhelm threatening to cut off my air supply.

He nodded, a sensual smile spreading over his lips and making my pulse accelerate even more. He really was devastatingly handsome when he smiled, even if the joke was on me when he replied. 'Do not concern yourself,' he said, having to raise his voice as the noise from the blades increased. 'You will not have to pilot it.'

I choked out a laugh. 'Good to know,' I murmured.

'And it is the fastest and safest way to travel through the city,' he added.

'Fair point,' I said, starting to babble. 'I've only been in Naples for two days, but I've already figured out the only rule drivers observe here is, "He who beeps loudest has right of way."'

He grinned, the wind whipping his dark hair around

his head and making my heart swell alongside my excitement. 'You see, Mia, you are already a native.'

Exhilaration made my heart punch my ribs as we boarded the chopper together. Even though I knew his approval shouldn't matter to me so much, somehow it did.

He strapped me in and handed me a pair of headphones before taking the seat beside me. I could hear him talking to the pilot in Italian, the deafening noise muffled by the headphones. Then we lifted into the night sky.

Tears stung my eyes and my heart rose to slam into my throat as I spotted the yacht in the distance, where Evie and her friends would probably be partying until dawn. The helicopter wheeled around to travel across the city, low enough for me to spot the faded neoclassical grandeur and labyrinthine alleyways of the Centro Storico we'd explored while searching for the perfect party outfits, the pavement cafes along the Via Francesco Caracciolo where we'd dined on pasta, and even Bagno Elena nestled between two headlands—the town beach where we had spent the day yesterday making the most of our fifteen-euro loungers.

The reminder of how far removed my world was from Vito's as the chopper climbed over the hills of the elegant Chiaia neighbourhood had apprehension pressing against my throat again.

I crossed my legs and tried to tug down the hem of my mini-dress. Vito's large palm settled on my bare knee, and sensation sprinted up my leg to settle in my sex.

'*Calmati*, Mia,' he said, and although I didn't understand Italian, I realised he was trying to quell my anxiety.

I glanced at him, my heart throbbing.

Stop panicking, Mia, and enjoy this.

What exactly was I getting so anxious about? This

was a one-night hookup, something I'd missed out on all through my teens because I'd had so many other responsibilities. And it promised to be a spectacular one at that.

And what was so scary about meeting a man who knew what he wanted—namely, me—and wasn't afraid to go after it? His confidence and no-nonsense approach to hooking up ought to fill me with confidence, too. Why shouldn't I be as bold as he was tonight, as badass as I'd always wanted to be? The only thing I had to lose was my vanilla sex life.

I'd spent my whole life denying my own needs to please other people and always do the sensible thing, but I'd made a promise to myself, and Evie, after I'd told Dave to take a hike. I was going to stop being so cautious.

No regrets Mia, not tonight. You've already had too many of those.

My heart danced and my clit throbbed harder as my needy senses went into a tailspin, almost as fast and giddy as the chopper's blades.

Tonight, I planned to party with a panther, escape into his fantasy world, get my money's worth out of this ridiculously expensive dress, and finally allow myself to be young and wild and impulsive for the first time in my life.

CHAPTER THREE

Vito

SHE DOES NOT know who I am...the boss of the most powerful Mafia syndicate in Campania.

The thought was like a shot of adrenaline, mainlining through my bloodstream as I felt Mia Taylor's toned thigh tremble beneath my palm. The helicopter climbed towards the villa, the city laid out below us, so much of which I now owned.

This stunning creature had no idea of the things I had done to survive, and then to prosper. She had no reason to fear me or appease me. Excitement pulsed in my groin at the memory of her quick wit, and her innocent fury at my teasing—and the way her breath had gushed against my neck in staggered gasps. Then her lips had moulded to mine while I devoured that provocative mouth and explored her curves.

I'd had my consigliere, Gattuso, do a background check on Mia as soon as I had spotted her amongst the other guests lining up on the dock, to ensure her appearance was not a honey trap set by the authorities or my half brother, Dante. It would be just like that bastard to use a woman to get to me.

But once Gattuso had confirmed she was a tourist from London, and a schoolteacher no less, the hunger to see those bright green eyes daze with lust, to inhale the scent of her arousal and feel her thighs wrap around my waist while I thrust into her willing body, had become impossible to ignore.

I had been patient for months, denied the pleasures I had once taken for granted, forced to focus on defeating Dante and his threat to the Rocco empire. But I had been on the hunt for a woman tonight, as living like a monk had only increased my frustration.

Gattuso, of course, had advised against a hookup with a hot tourist. But then, Gattuso had always been a killjoy—a man who had never understood the main upside of this life was to take what you wanted, whenever you wanted it. So what if we were in a turf war with my half brother? We were winning. And there was no purpose to fighting a war if you could not enjoy the spoils.

A heavy sigh echoed in my headphones, the staggered awe of the girl beside me like a vindication of all I had suffered and survived to get to this moment in time. In charge of my own destiny. Able to destroy any bastard who dared take it from me.

This night would be a reward for all the battles fought and won in the last six months. Dante had sensed a weakness and tried to exploit it. But he had soon discovered his mistake—that the power vacuum he had anticipated after our father's death two years ago had never existed.

A price had been paid in good men and money while he challenged my authority. But we had victory within our grasp now. And I was ready to celebrate. But I was bored with women who threw themselves at me, drawn to the danger and power of my position.

Mia Taylor—with her spectacular breasts, the shocked awe in her eyes when our gazes had first connected tonight and her innocent awareness—was the perfect way to ease the throbbing in my cock caused by being too long without a woman. She had also been a delightful surprise. Provocative and seductive but also unconventional and unaware of her charms.

When was the last time I had taken a woman who saw me as a man instead of the head of a criminal empire? Never, certainly not since I had hit puberty and been declared the rightful heir and then the underboss of the Rocco Syndicate.

Tonight, I couldn't imagine anything hotter than tasting this woman, tormenting her, taming her—as nothing more than a man.

We would part ways as soon as dawn broke. I was not in the market for anything permanent. I trusted no one entirely, not even Gattuso. But I intended to ensure, when I did let Mia go, she would never forget me.

As the helicopter circled the estate in Naples, I heard Mia's sharp intake of breath as she absorbed the sight of the city below. The blanket of lights which covered the headland, the terracotta rooftops and terraces stacked on the hillside, the dark lump of Capri in the distance—and a few miles to the west, Isla Donna, the island fortress I had called home ever since my father had rescued me from my stepfather at my mother's graveside.

'The city's so beautiful,' she whispered.

'It is certainly something.' I let out a raw laugh at her naïveté and inhaled her scent—sultry spice and fresh blooms—as the helicopter settled on the front lawn. The heat in my groin surged.

Naples and my life here hadn't been beautiful, it had been dangerous and terrifying—the scrabble for survival harder than elsewhere because violence and death lurked around every corner when you knew where to look. And if you didn't have power, you had nothing.

I had once been powerless, which was why I would stop at nothing to ensure I was never powerless again.

But nothing could make you feel more alive than winning that fight. Except maybe the moment of climax inside a woman, which the French called *la petite mort*.

I was too hard, too volatile, too dominant to want more than sex from a woman like her—who for all her courage was gullible and naive—but I knew how to make her come until she screamed.

She had taken a risk tonight, not knowing who I was. A man who commanded an empire and could have any woman he wanted with the snap of his fingers. But tonight, I wanted her, with a fever that surprised me.

It wasn't about this girl. However stunning and unusual she was, she wasn't special. How could she be, when she wasn't even Italian—and knew nothing of my world? But the thought of seducing her, a sweet, ordinary schoolteacher—when I had been the worst student imaginable—added a layer of irony that only made me want her more.

I had seen the naked hunger she couldn't disguise— felt the attraction spark between us when our gazes had locked—and enjoyed immensely her attempts to hold her own against me. And the way she responded to me—without holding anything back—only added more potential to a night which was already as hot as it was intriguing.

Mia would be my gift to myself for six months of frustration and provocation. One long, hot night of pleasure, while I made my stunning little English schoolteacher beg for release.

CHAPTER FOUR

Mia

I watched, open-mouthed, as the helicopter touched down inside the grounds of a magnificent walled estate perched above the city.

From the bus tour I had done with Evie and our friends on our first evening in the city, I knew Naples had a history of occupation, and its architecture reflected that—from elaborately decorated Baroque churches to the Renaissance finery and Mediterranean practicality of the city's historic homes—but as Vito escorted me down the steps of the helicopter, and I got my first look at the house, I'd never seen a building here as elaborate or well maintained.

Four stories of ornate plaster were lit by torches and covered in bougainvillea, a selection of wrought-iron balconies and tall, mullioned windows adding to its imposing grandeur. He had referred to his home as a villa, but the building's neoclassical splendour made it look more like a palace.

Becca had said Vito was phenomenally rich, but I hadn't expected anything this elegant or awe-inspiring.

We walked up the marble staircase at the front of the

house, which led to an arched entrance flanked by Doric columns and two stone lions, almost as striking as their owner.

Three men appeared from inside the house.

Vito spoke to them in Italian. All three of them bowed while one replied, his tone low with deference, '*Si*, Don Vito, *mio padrino...*'

Vito exuded power and arrogance, but as he led me past his staff, their subservience was a little unnerving… not to mention weirdly hot. Who knew I had a thing for powerful men?

'Why did he call you *padrino*?' I asked, recalling how Lorenzo, the bodyguard on the boat, had addressed him the same way.

Vito headed through the main entrance. 'It is from respect,' he said as I rushed to keep up with him.

Okay, what?

Was Vito some kind of prince? I knew Italy had become a republic in the forties and the state no longer recognised the titles of the aristocracy—but according to our bus tour, there were still aristocratic families that owned estates in the region.

Two people appeared in the mansion's cavernous entrance hall to greet us. An older woman dressed in black and a man in a linen suit. I recognised him from the men surrounding Vito when he'd given me 'the look'.

Again, they both bowed and addressed him as Don Vito. After a brief exchange in Italian with the woman, Vito turned to me.

Tugging me close, he lifted my hand to his lips and pressed a kiss to my knuckles, his eyes dark with the same hunger that had been burning inside me since 'the look'.

'Do you wish to eat?' he asked.

I shook my head, surprised he had offered—almost as if this were a date instead of a booty call—but knowing I was way too hyper to eat anything.

'No, I'm not hungry,' I said.

His gaze raked over me, the fierce approval in those pure blue eyes making me dizzy.

'*Bene*,' he said. 'There is only one thing I am hungry for too, and it is not food.'

The intense expression made his meaning clear and a wave of adrenaline hurtled through my system. He turned back to his staff and dismissed them both.

But while the woman disappeared again, the man spoke—his voice low with what sounded like concern or even disapproval as his gaze flicked to me.

Although Vito didn't raise his voice, I could hear the sharp reprimand in the tone when he replied in Italian. The man had obviously heard it too, because his colour heightened, but instead of arguing the point, he only nodded, bowed again, then left us, too.

'Is there… Is there a problem with me being here?' I asked.

'The only problem is that you are not naked yet,' he said, his voice rough with amusement.

'You're not very subtle,' I murmured, suddenly needing to slow him down just a little. I knew tonight was about hunger, passion, getting off, and I was more than okay with that. But I didn't want this to be over too soon. And me to be left feeling unsatisfied, or worse, used. Because I'd already had enough of that feeling to last me a lifetime.

But instead of taking the hint, he chuckled. 'Subtlety is not one of my virtues,' he declared. 'But when I make you come until you scream my name, you will not be complaining,' he finished, marching down the entrance hall and then taking the wide, sweeping staircase to the next floor.

Giddy excitement raced through me as I was dragged along in his wake. 'And super arrogant to boot,' I added, trying to sound as if I wasn't already melting into a puddle of pheromones at his demanding tone.

When had I ever met a man who took what he wanted without bothering to wait for an invitation? On the one hand, it ought to be a turn-off. I wasn't used to being told what to do. On the other, this was already the hottest night of my life. Bar none.

He pushed open a door at the end of the landing and tugged me into a huge room, with a balcony at the far end which looked out over the gardens and the city below. The view was breathtaking, but that wasn't why I was struggling to breathe when he let go of my hand, strolled across the expanse of silk carpet and opened the terrace doors onto the night.

A scented breeze brushed over my exposed skin, which, thanks to my mini-dress, was a lot.

Instead of returning to me, he sat in an upholstered chair that looked antique, crossed his ankle over the other knee, and smiled at me, the feral light in his eyes as tempting as it was intimidating.

'My arrogance is part of my charm, Mia,' he said before flicking his index finger to indicate my dress. 'It is time for you to show me everything that is under that dress.'

'But… I'm…' The words seized in my throat as I stalled. I'd never done a striptease before, and as bold as I'd felt up to now, I was suddenly struggling with a serious case of performance anxiety. '*Really*?' I managed. 'That's not very seductive…'

'And yet you are already wet for me,' he replied.

My thighs quivered as the evening breeze chose that precise moment to make me aware of how damp I was. For him.

'How do you know that?' I blurted out, challenging him to cover my mortification.

He crooked his finger at me. 'Come.'

I walked towards him, aware of the swollen spot between my thighs every step of the way. He unfolded his legs and spread his knees. Placing a hand on my hip, he positioned me between his muscular thighs.

Every part of me trembled as he tucked a knuckle under my chin and forced my gaze to his. 'If I find that you are wet, Mia, I will have to punish you for lying.'

My eyes widened as the need pulsed and throbbed between my legs. His hand trailed under the hem of my dress. He cupped me to run his finger along the seam of my sex.

I sobbed and grabbed hold of his shoulders in a desperate attempt not to collapse into a heap, his dominating caress so sure, so entitled it was electrifying. His knuckle brushed my clitoris, and I bucked against his hold, shocked by the brutal sensations radiating outwards. Already.

But just as I felt myself shooting towards orgasm, he denied me the touch I needed and gave my bare buttock a stinging slap.

I jolted upright. 'You bastard,' I managed, my throat dry.

'I said you would be punished,' he said, his eyes dark with hunger and bright with satisfaction.

'I never said I wasn't aroused…*specifically*,' I said, trying to justify myself but losing ground fast. I wanted what he was offering, his power and dominance pushing me out of my comfort zone in the most delicious way possible. I'd never been so close to orgasm before so quickly.

'Then do as I demand,' he said.

'I don't like being ordered about.'

'Yes, you do…' He brought his finger to his lips, my juices glistening in the moonlight and calling me a liar, then sucked his fingertip. 'Delicious,' he murmured, the gruff approval making need grip me again. 'Take off the dress so I can feast on you, Mia.'

I shuddered as heat poured through me—his dictatorial tone as hot as that sure, entitled caress.

A part of me knew I really ought to tell him no. I was a feminist, which meant I shouldn't be turned on by his bossy tone, or that stinging slap. But in that moment, my poor neglected libido was making all my decisions for me.

Dave had never gone down on me, because he said he found it repulsive. So I'd locked that desire away with all the others. But Vito didn't just look like he wanted to eat me. He looked as if he would punish me again if I didn't let him…

I lifted the dress over my head and threw it away, feeling bold, and more belligerent myself. No point in being coy, or contrary. I could subjugate my equal rights for one night, for the greater good—i.e., discovering what it was like to have a man actually *want* to fulfil my biggest sexual fantasy.

'*Brava ragazza*,' he said, the low tone and that fierce gaze raking over my breasts and making me painfully aware of my nipples poking the red lace. He inclined his head. 'The bra,' he announced. 'Lose it.'

I didn't need to be asked twice. I reached behind me but struggled to unclip the hook. It took me a few painful seconds, but he made no move to help me. Once I'd finally unclipped the bra and let it drop, I was shaking—with need or mortification, or possibly both.

But then he adjusted his trousers and unzipped himself to reveal a pair of black stretch boxers with an obscene bulge which had to be the thick ridge I had felt earlier.

Desire swelled and throbbed, my need painful as my sex ached with emptiness—the desperation to feel that bulge inside me all I could focus on.

Before I had a chance to contemplate how quickly I was losing every one of my inhibitions, he curled a hand around my waist and tugged me closer. He blew across my bare nipple. My back arched, offering the swollen peak to him.

He licked at the tip, swirled his tongue around the edge. I thrust my fingers into his hair. But before I could start begging—just as he had said I would—he reared back, dislodging my hands.

'Not yet,' he said, but I could see he had lost that cast-iron control for a moment, and I felt the heady surge of triumph in our erotic battle of wills.

'Hold on to my right shoulder,' he said. I did as I was told, but before I could figure out why, he clasped my right thigh and hooked it over his left shoulder.

I had to hold on to him so I wouldn't fall over. My position was impossibly vulnerable, my sex level with his face. Before I could panic or worry about whether I had the strength to stay upright in this position, he ran his nose up my inner thigh, then sank his teeth into the front of my thong and tore it free.

I was still reeling with shock, still holding on to him for dear life, my whole body quivering with need, when he ran his tongue over the folds of my sex.

I moaned, stunned by the sensation. Wet and firm, his tongue felt incredible as he explored in rough, raw strokes, lapping at my folds, stirring the intense pleasure to life in vicious waves. He gripped my thigh, positioning me so that I had no choice but to open myself completely to his marauding mouth.

I gasped, writhed, forcing myself into the heat. I felt dazed, weightless, drifting into another realm, where only the pleasure mattered. I rode the slick waves starting to consume me. Then he used his thumb to expose the hot button at the top of my clitoris and closed his lips over it to suckle me.

The pleasure exploded in glittering shards, racing along my nerve endings, blooming outwards in throbbing euphoria—too bright, too brutal, too overwhelming… The orgasm ripped through me but seemed to last for an eternity. Finally he released me from its grip and gently lowered my leg back to the floor.

I felt the ache in my thigh muscles from the position he'd held me in. And the much greater ache in my sex—the desperation to be filled painful now—as he stood to tower over me and cradled my cheek.

'*Brava*, Mia,' he murmured, the smugness in his tone bearable because of the approval. Then he clasped my neck and kissed me—forceful and possessive.

I could taste myself on his lips. Spicy and erotic—and not at all repulsive.

But I was still shaking, the afterglow shimmering through me, when the emotion of it all blindsided me.

I'd never had an orgasm with Dave. The man I'd intended to marry. The man I had convinced myself I loved—because he was convenient and safe. And now this man, who I didn't even know, and who I already suspected was the opposite of safe, had given me something I would always cherish.

'Thank you,' I mumbled, the tears stinging my eyes at the thought of that girl who had always settled for less far too easily.

'*Prego*,' he murmured, but his husky chuckle made me feel foolish. What was I getting so overemotional about?

I tried to draw away from him, but he gripped my arm, forcing me to meet his gaze.

'The night is not over, Mia,' he said, the promise in his eyes as intoxicating as that brutal blue gaze, so hot it burned. 'You respond to me very well, and you come so beautifully. I will want to make you come many times before morning.'

He was talking about sex, but somehow it sounded like so much more.

Shame washed over me, and embarrassment.

Could he see how desperate I had always been to be desired, to be touched, to be devoured? Even to be dominated? And why did the thought we had only tonight make regret pulse in my chest?

I didn't have a chance to dwell on my reaction, though, when he ran his thumb across my lower lip. 'I want this beautiful mouth on my cock,' he said, as direct as always. 'But first I must fuck you.'

I blushed at his bluntness, but felt stupidly grateful to him for getting our booty call back on track. I wanted both those things, too. Oral sex had always been a chore up to now. But not anymore. I had no idea how I was going to accommodate his huge cock, which looked massive even disguised by his boxers. But I knew I wanted to try.

I nodded and reached for him, running my hand over

the thick ridge through the cloth, gauging the size, the firmness.

He grabbed my wrist and jerked back, preventing me from caressing him. 'I am too close,' he groaned.

Excitement surged on a wave of achievement, that I had done this to such a powerful man.

He kissed my fingers, then led me through the salon and into a bedroom. A large king-size bed dominated the luxuriously furnished room, moonlight covering the satin sheets in a silvery glow.

Releasing me, he sat to tug off his shoes, then stood and thrust down his trousers and boxers. The enormous erection sprang out, reaching skyward, thick and hard and heavily engorged. I swallowed, the lump of emotion in my throat joined by stunned arousal.

I watched as he tugged his T-shirt over his head until he stood naked.

The scars and tattoos that adorned his body only enhanced his dangerous beauty. My avaricious gaze skated over the dark hair covering the ink on his chest, the necklace of thorns drawn around his collarbones, the broad shoulders and biceps where more ink swirled.

But once my gaze had drifted past stacked abs, and the spectacular V defining his hip bones, it snagged again on his thrusting cock, so long, so hard, the bulbous head glistening with pre-cum. He gripped himself and slid his fist up and down, tugging in rough strokes.

'You like what you see, Mia?' he asked.

I nodded, totally mute now. My throat was as raw as the rest of me, my sex so swollen it felt as if I had a bowling ball between my thighs.

He sat down on the bed and gripped my wrist, then

pulled me towards him. 'You must ride it,' he said, the amused tone husky with need.

I nodded again. He chuckled, the rough sound scraping across my nerve endings.

'Then take off the shoes and mount me.'

The… *What?* I glanced down, realising all this time I had been naked but still wearing the heels.

I blushed, but it took me less than a second to toe off the shoes. He held my arm as I climbed onto the bed, placing my hands on his shoulders, aware of the thick erection brushing my inner thigh.

He cupped my chin and kissed me again as he grasped my hip in his other hand, positioning me. His thumb slid along the seam of my sex, making me jump slightly as he stroked my tender clit. He laughed, but the sound was thick with desire, the thread of emotion still there between us. Holding himself, he guided me down until the head spread the lips of my sex. I sucked in a breath, the penetration already immense. But the desire to take more, to take all of him, was overwhelming.

The slickness of my orgasm eased his way, until I was sitting on his lap, his huge cock stretching me unbearably. I panted, shifted, trying to ease the sensation. He held me in place and kissed me again, his tongue thrusting deep into my mouth, owning me, insisting I adjust to the brutal invasion.

The fog of desire descended over me, my mind hazy with lust, the passion pressing against me. I could feel the throb of his cock inside me, buried to the hilt.

He dragged his mouth away, ending the kiss. Then he rasped, 'You are so tight. You must move, Mia—or I will finish before you.'

Grasping my bottom in rough hands, he lifted me,

easing the pressure at last as the erection massaged my inner walls. I clung to his shoulders, letting him drag me down, slowly establishing a brutal rhythm of deep thrusts.

Pleasure bloomed and surged in devastating waves. I clung to him, moving with him now, using my knees for leverage. The sensations built, merging, blending, becoming so intense I couldn't breathe.

His grunts matched my sobs. I felt conquered, owned, forced into a maelstrom I couldn't control. The pleasure became vicious and all-consuming, rising, building, draining.

'I can't come…' I moaned, desperate to reach that final peak so I could escape the terrifying storm of sensations battering me, my body trapped in a vortex of pleasure too tumultuous to bear.

'You must…' he demanded, then found the place where our bodies joined and stroked the perfect spot as he impaled me one last time.

The pleasure crested like a tsunami, tearing free, ripping me apart as I screamed.

'Vito!'

The orgasm slammed into me, shattering, surreal, as he threw back his head and roared his own release—his hot seed branding my insides.

I collapsed onto his shoulder, shaking. His arms wrapped around me, holding me up, holding me close. His face pressed into my hair, our shattered breathing the only sound but for the distant beep of car horns and the buzz of the nighttime city which drifted in on the breeze.

My heart was still thundering, my sex sore from the pounding he'd given it, my shattered senses scattered. The afterglow shimmered around me like a golden cloud—

glittering and glorious—while the sultry air brushed over my damp skin.

I'd never made love like that before, the need so basic, so elemental, so wild and untamed, and it had been magnificent. But when his hand brushed down my spine to clasp my bottom, I felt the slickness between my thighs.

I bolted upright. Reality returned in a rush of panic, accompanied by the slap of shame. The condoms Evie had bought me at the airport—as a joke—were still tucked into the purse Vito had handed to the bodyguard on the boat. Which the guard had never handed back to me, I realised now, too late.

'Shit!' I climbed off him, frantic.

How could I have been so reckless, so stupid? This wasn't me. I always planned ahead. I wasn't spontaneous or impulsive. And while doing what I wanted for once without thinking of the consequences had been beyond exciting, now I was paying the price.

I'd had unprotected sex, with a stranger… *What the hell?* It was exactly the sort of thing my mum had done to get pregnant with me.

'I have to go,' I said, rushing over to grab my dress and bra from the floor where I'd tossed them away. 'I need to find my purse.' How the heck was I going to get morning-after medication in Italy?

'Hey! Mia.' He stood and strode towards me, comfortable in his nakedness.

He snagged my wrist, preventing me from putting on the dress. The shiver of sensation darting up my arm was nothing compared to the deep pulse in my sex at the sight of him—so tall, so fit, so gorgeous. Even flaccid, his cock looked impressive.

'You cannot leave,' he said, his brow furrowing. 'The night is not over. And your purse will be safe until morning.'

'But we didn't use any protection,' I blurted out. 'I have condoms in my purse, but I totally forgot about it…about them. Everything was just so…*hot*. I've never done it before without protection.' Not even with Dave, I thought miserably, because sex had never been this hot or spontaneous with him. 'And I just didn't stop to think, so I have to…'

'Shhh…' He pressed a finger to my lips to stop the babble of panic in its tracks. 'I am healthy. This is a first for me also.'

My panic downgraded a notch. But there was still the massive problem of pregnancy.

'I'm so sorry, I'm not on the pill…' I managed, feeling so gauche and unsophisticated having to make the admission. If he hadn't guessed already I was a hookup virgin, he would certainly know now. 'I should have said something, I know, but…'

He stroked his thumb across my lips, silencing me again. But his expression barely changed, until his lips twisted in a sensual smile. To my astonishment, he didn't look shocked or horrified at my confession. Instead, his eyes became hooded with what I now recognised as desire.

'I like imagining this body pregnant with my child…' he murmured, running his palm down to cup my breast and thumb the nipple.

'What…?' I croaked, shocked he could find the prospect arousing.

'Your breasts would become so sensitive.'

I shuddered, the streak of heat firing deep into my abdomen as he pinched my nipple, just hard enough to make sensation dart down to my core, heady and all-consuming.

'Your belly where my child would grow would brand you as mine,' he rumbled, his voice rich with the possessiveness I had noticed before.

I groaned, the picture he was painting both insane and wildly erotic.

Did he have some kind of fetish about pregnancy? I couldn't process the thought when he cupped my sex as if it belonged to him, his fingers stroking, delving. I had to clasp his forearm, his touch too much, the tenderness there making me ache even as I wanted to ride his hand.

He clasped my neck with his other hand, dragged me close to press his lips to the pulse point under my ear.

'It is making me want you again...' he murmured, caressing the soft skin with those demanding lips as his fingers delved and probed again, rubbing the hot, sweet spot he had already feasted on.

I let out a staggered groan, forced to drop the dress, to cling to those broad shoulders as he turned the tenderness to hard, driving need.

'Do not worry. If there is a baby, I will protect it...' he said. 'And you.'

My mind struggled to make sense of what he was saying as I plummeted head first into that hot vat of bliss all over again.

Even though I knew in some corner of my mind—where I could still process coherent thought—what he was saying was all wrong...because we'd only just met, and a pregnancy would be a disaster...his words—so gruff and sure and protective—were also impossibly arousing.

'We will not take the risk again,' he said, scooping me into his arms and striding back to the bed. After placing me on the satin sheets, he produced a box of condoms from the bedside table and made short work of sheathing the already thickening erection. Apparently he was as turned on as I was by the thought of an unplanned pregnancy.

What the hell?

But as he climbed on the bed and pressed my knees wide, I was swept away on a new wave of adrenaline, the endorphin high making coherent thought impossible. I flinched as he sank into me in one sure, devastating thrust, filling me to bursting again. The penetration was as immense as before. He brushed the sweaty hair back from my forehead and kissed me hard on the lips while I adjusted to the devastating feel of having him inside me again, lodged deep.

'But if fate gives us a baby—we will honour it,' he declared.

I found myself nodding dumbly, not really having any clue what he meant… He couldn't *want* to become a father in these circumstances, with a woman he'd hooked up with for a single night. But I couldn't think about it now, as he began to move, rolling his hips out and back, conquering every part of me and claiming me as his.

I lifted my hips to meet his devastating thrusts, and decided I would have to think about it all tomorrow. Because tonight, all I could do was ride the whirlwind once more.

Vito

I worked her tight flesh in vicious strokes until the climax hit me, the grip of the orgasm as agonising as it was euphoric, rolling through my body like a summer storm. Wild, free and devastating.

She groaned, her hands clinging to my shoulders, her body milking me. Her face was a picture of shock and awe before I collapsed into her arms.

I braced my hands on the bed, pushed myself back so as not to crush her under my weight. But my arms were shaking, my muscles straining as I pulled out of her with difficulty and rolled to flop onto the bed beside her.

I felt drained, exhausted. I'd never had a climax like it. Make that two climaxes like it. And yet already, I could feel my cock twitching again, the heavy weight in my groin still not satisfied as I turned my head to find her staring back at me, those mossy-green eyes dazed.

I reached out to cradle her cheek and sink my fingers into her wild hair. I dragged her close to capture those plump lips and claim them again. Then I trailed my hand down to cup her full breast, thumb the nipple, still rigid and begging for my mouth.

I swallowed heavily, my cock thickening again—wanting more, when it should already have had enough.

She clasped my wrist, then blinked. Her eyes widened as she glanced down and spotted my eager cock.

'Didn't you come?' she asked, sounding concerned.

I let out a gruff laugh, enjoying her expression. How could she be so hot and yet also so unsure? In a way, though, her innocence was strangely beguiling. Gullibility was not something I had ever valued before now. In fact, normally I would happily exploit it. But on her it was almost like a strength instead of a weakness, a shield against the darkness.

I shook off the dumb notion—clearly the stress of the last few months had taken a bigger toll than I had realised. But my voice was rough with an emotion I didn't like when I spoke. 'Yes. But my cock has other ideas,' I said, being deliberately crude.

I dragged the sheet up and over us both, placed my hand behind my head and willed my cock to behave.

Dio. What the hell was happening to me? I enjoyed sex as much as the next man, probably more. It had always been a valuable stress release from the danger I lived in. But I had never been insatiable. Had never felt this grinding hunger to possess a woman so completely, even the prospect of a pregnancy hadn't deterred me—or disgusted me, as it should.

In fact, when she revealed she wasn't on the pill, and I had realised I hadn't even thought of protection myself—something I had never forgotten before—my first reaction had been a surge of adrenaline so intense it had blindsided me. The elemental desire to mark her as mine, to see her body grow and change as it nurtured my seed, had been nothing short of animalistic. And so erotic, I'd known I had to have her again or die.

But even now, it didn't feel like we were done—which was almost as concerning as my dumb decision to let her ride me bareback.

I should have her escorted back to her hotel. I had never brought a woman to the palazzo before—which was why Gattuso had been so concerned when we had arrived. The villa was my stronghold and the base of my operations in Naples. I kept the estate heavily guarded, and the only people I allowed into the house itself were people I paid well for their loyalty. Not a one-night hookup who did not even know who I was.

Normally I would take a woman I wanted to my cabin on the yacht. Because then I could leave them there at my convenience… I didn't sleep much, and rarely at night. It was in the dark that danger lurked. I had learnt this the hard way as a boy… And I did not need a woman in my bed for anything other than sex. Nighttime was when I needed to be at my most alert.

But as she lay silently beside me, just listening to her breathing, knowing she was there felt good. So when she lifted the sheet, clearly intending to slip away from me again, I found myself reaching out to grasp her wrist.

Don't leave me.

The request almost slipped out, but I bit it back, horrified it had sprung into my head in the first place. Where had that come from? I had not needed anyone—and certainly not a woman—since I had lost my mother.

'Where are you going?' I demanded more roughly than I had intended when I saw her flinch.

'I don't… I don't think I can take you again so soon,' she murmured, clearly referring to my needy cock, which still hadn't got the message.

I dragged her back towards me and kissed her nose, touched by her bluntness and enjoying her latest show of independence. Funny, I had never found honesty a turn-on before now either, but with her it was. Women were too willing to do as I asked of them, especially since I had become a don. As a result, my sex life had become jaded… I was prepared to use force in my business, but it was not something which had ever excited me in bed. I didn't trade protection or anything else for sex. My father, Don Salvatore, had taught me there was a code with women, as with everything else. A code of honour that should not be broken.

I had thought his code foolish as a teenager. In fact, it had angered me. Because my mother had broken the code—by not honouring their marriage—and he had always refused to condemn her for it. She had not shown loyalty to my father or the family, when she had run from him and taken me with her. And left us both at the mercy of a man who had enjoyed hurting us.

I pushed the thoughts of my past to one side. It had no place here. Was this the reason for my foolish desire to keep Mia close tonight? A layover from my screwed-up childhood?

But as my gaze sank to her breasts, plump and round, the freckles across her cleavage visible in the moonlight, my erection swelled. I almost sighed with relief. This was about sex, nothing more. And being too long without a woman. Mia and I were extraordinarily compatible, and the fact she had no idea who I was added novelty to this encounter, which made the sex more addictive.

'Stay until morning…' I demanded.

Once dawn broke, I would have had my fill of her, and any thoughts about my past would be locked away again. I was not that frightened child anymore. I was a man who could command an army. An army that had won the war to regain all my father's territory—when Dante had tried to encroach on it after his death.

She stared back at me, those wide, guileless eyes a misty emerald in the moonlight, the scent of her intoxicating as she considered my proposal. As I waited for her answer, I had the unsettling thought maybe my desire for her to say yes was about more than just sex. My heart throbbed in my throat, the sense of anticipation as rare as it was disturbing.

'Okay,' she said, blushing prettily, clearly having surprised herself.

Relief coursed through me, but I forced myself not to show it.

'But can I have a shower?' she asked.

I laughed, breaking the tension. *Dio*, but she was adorable. I kept a firm grip on her wrist and tugged her to me until I could hook my leg over hers and make her aware of my growing need.

'Yes, but only if I can join you.' I pressed a finger to her lower lip, excitement surging when she nipped the tip. 'I still want to feel these lips wrapped around my cock.'

Her mouth curved in a sensual smile as she stretched against me—bold and beautiful. And then she licked her lips, and the searing heat in her gaze made my cock throb back to full mast.

'All right,' she replied, her voice as husky as mine. 'If you insist.'

'I do,' I said.

But just as I reached for her, preparing to make her pay for her earlier defiance, she slipped out of my arms, scrambled off the bed and darted towards the bathroom.

'But you'll have to catch me first,' she shouted over her shoulder.

I swore in Italian as I watched her streak off, her bare butt bobbing in the moonlight, my cock hardening even more. I jumped from the bed, determined to catch her—but as I chased after her, her playful laughs released the knot in my chest which had been there for months, maybe even years.

Once I had caught her and she was on her knees, that succulent mouth caressing my aching cock, her eyes dazed with lust, my mind shattering with the intensity of the orgasm approaching, I was forced to acknowledge I had never had a more erotic experience in my life...

But later, as I drifted into a deep sleep and I tightened my arms around her, a disturbing thought consumed me. What if one night with this woman was not enough, and I was not ready to let her go in the morning?

CHAPTER FIVE

Mia

MY EYES JERKED OPEN, my body nestled against something solid, and warm—that smelt of oranges and soap and sex.

Vito. My billionaire booty call.

A dreamy smile tugged at my lips as I snuggled into his delicious scent, recalling all the ways we'd made love during the night. *God.* It had been so intense. Like something out of a gloriously filthy erotic dream. He'd woken me several times, coaxing, demanding, determined, driving me to orgasm again and again, until we'd both collapsed for the last time at around three a.m.

I blinked, trying to clear my head of the weird dream I'd been having of my mum cooking popcorn—the kernels bursting around me on the stove—while Vito cradled me in his arms, his demanding erection prodding my bottom.

I wriggled, realising the stiff bar nestled against my bum was not a dream. I could hear his heavy breathing against my ear, his face buried in my hair, and his forearm wrapped around my waist.

My one-night lover was still fast asleep. But his erection had a mind of its own.

I smiled even as the sharp pang returned at the thought that our night was nearly over. Because I could see the rosy dawn through the balcony doors, bleeding into the night sky on the horizon.

But then a stream of muffled pops had me lifting onto my elbows. What on earth was that noise? Was someone *actually* making popcorn?

Vito's forearm tensed under my breasts as a shout echoed from the garden below us. He shot upright—instantly wide awake. I glanced round, still groggy and confused, when I registered his expression—harsh and unyielding.

The popping noises returned.

'What is that?' I asked.

Swearing in Italian, he flung the sheet off and leapt from the bed naked.

'Under the bed. *Now*,' he shouted as he pulled on his boxers.

Three men burst into the suite—the one who had greeted us in the hallway last night and two others. All three of them were carrying assault rifles.

I was still reeling from the sight of the terrifying weapons, which I'd only ever seen before in movies, when one of them shouted to Vito in Italian and threw him another gun—which he caught one-handed.

Too terrified to move, I grasped the sheet to cover my nakedness, although I was shaking so hard with shock I could barely keep hold of it. Another series of pops, louder this time, was accompanied by the sound of glass shattering and the thunk, thunk, thunk of something hitting the bedroom's back wall.

'Mia!' Vito yelled my name, then dived across the bed to cover me. His body spasmed as he hissed in pain right next to my ear. The men who had entered the suite charged past us and stood in front of the bed like a wall, the rat-a-tat-tat of their guns firing into the night.

The scent of something burning, the flashes of light and those ominous popping sounds became so overwhelming I had to cover my ears. The surge of panic was so huge it felt like a rope around my neck, even as Vito's body cocooned mine. He groaned, then his weight lifted off me. He staggered, but then he grabbed my arm, dipped down and hefted me onto his shoulder, gathering the sheet with me.

Disorientated and dazed, I blinked at the red stain blooming against the white linen sheet draped over his back. I couldn't seem to focus as the carpet drifted past under his feet, aware of his shoulder digging into my stomach. The sheet had dropped, exposing my breasts. I was naked in front of all these men with guns, but my mind was numb.

Vito strode from the room, then kicked open the main door to the suite. He took the stairs down to the lobby two at a time with me bouncing on his shoulder. I could hear my heart thundering and the chaos around us. The cacophony of noise was almost as terrifying as the sticky red stain, which was growing on the sheet.

Was he bleeding? Was I? Why couldn't I feel anything?

Crashing, banging, popping and the acrid scent of burning sulphur surrounded us like some horrifying funfair ride as I rode his shoulder, unable to move, scared to speak.

He shouted orders in rapid Italian to another group of men who had gathered in the main entrance hall. As they rushed to the front entrance, he dropped me on my feet. The bloodied sheet fell to the floor, leaving me naked, but I couldn't move, dazed by the adrenaline charging through my body. What was happening? In weird slow motion, he tucked the pistol he'd caught upstairs into the back of his shorts and then grabbed the sheet off the floor to drape it around me as if he were covering a child.

Only then did I notice the blood pumping from a wound on his shoulder.

'Vito, you're bleeding!' I whispered, the words like sandpaper against my throat, the noose of panic tightening around my neck.

The housekeeper from the evening before appeared, also with a pistol in her hand. Lorenzo, the burly bodyguard who had been on the yacht, was right behind her, holding another of those fearsome assault rifles, his suit jacket gone, his shirt soaked through with sweat.

'*Gli uomini di Dante*,' he growled, then spat as if the name Dante was a bad taste in his mouth.

'*Padrino*!' the housekeeper gasped, then rushed forward. Dropping her gun into her apron pocket, she pulled out a roll of gauze. She tried to press the bandage to Vito's shoulder, but he brushed her away.

'*Dopo, non è niente*,' he said, the fury on his face sent shockwaves through me while he spoke to Lorenzo in Italian. His tone was low, but his voice was steady, his expression unmoved. He looked calm and cold, his features cast into harsh lines. I didn't recognise him as my seductive, playful, demanding lover.

The popping noises faded, drowned out by the sound of sirens in the distance.

Turning, he grasped my arms.

'You must leave Naples. Now. Lorenzo will take you to London. Never speak of this night to anyone.'

What? Why?

So many questions battered me. But I was shaking so hard I couldn't make sense of any of them.

'What about you?' I forced the question out past the ball of emotion cutting off my air supply. 'I don't want to leave without you…'

How could I leave him—when he was hurt?

I hadn't been hit. He'd saved me from the bullet and taken it himself. That was all my exhausted mind could seem to process.

He chuckled, which seemed incongruous in the circumstances. My confusion spiked—equal parts horror and humiliation. Why was he laughing? What was funny about this hideous situation?

'You cannot save me, Mia, when I do not wish to be saved.'

What did that even mean? Before I could gather myself enough to ask, he yanked me up on tiptoe.

Clasping me against him, he slanted his mouth across mine, capturing my gasp of surprise and the sob of need. His kiss was deep, forceful, demanding, pressing my breasts against his chest, almost as if he were branding me as his. The familiar heat—which he had conjured so effortlessly through the night—made my sex clench and release, my clitoris swell and ache, even as terror and confusion made my heart pound hard enough to be heard in Rome.

But when he thrust me away, the smile was still there, cynical and arrogant and cruel.

'It was only my cock that wanted you, Mia, nothing more.'

The words were harsh, insulting, making me feel used. I'd known this was a one-night stand, a booty call, a hookup…but it had felt like more when he'd worked me into a frenzy, when he'd held me in the moonlight, when he'd dived across the bed and yelled my name.

'Get her out. I don't want her here,' he said, addressing Lorenzo in English, clearly for my benefit.

'No, I won't leave…' I shouted, feeling bereft. But also confused. I couldn't leave him, not like this…

I tried to fight off Lorenzo's hold, desperate to know why Vito was treating me like this… But the bodyguard's arms were like iron bands as he dragged me towards the back of the house. I watched Vito stride towards the front entrance, drawing his gun from his shorts, his body magnificent and apparently unbowed by the injury.

He didn't look back. Not once.

Nausea rose up my throat, the metallic scent of blood from the sheet wrapped around me—Vito's blood—curdling my stomach, as I was bundled into a car. All the fight drained out of me. The strange sense of dislocation, of drifting outside my own body, was weirdly comforting, as if this was all happening to someone else. Someone that wasn't me.

Lorenzo shouted something in Italian to the driver. I could see police cars amassing outside the front gates as our car sped through the trees towards the back of the estate. A gate opened, and the car was ushered through. Then the driver put his foot down, throwing me back into the seat. Lorenzo grabbed my seat belt and put it on. Then he handed me my purse.

I looked inside it with shaking hands to find my phone gone.

'Where's my phone? I have to call my sister,' I managed, even now not quite able to forget my responsibility to her. 'She won't know where I am…' I managed.

We were all supposed to be catching our budget flight

together this evening, and my luggage was back at the hotel. Why had they taken my phone?

'Don Vito wants you gone,' he said, reiterating his boss's brutal request. 'She will be informed you have left early… I will give you your phone when we reach London.'

I didn't object, because I didn't have the strength to argue with him. In fact, I was unable to feel anything now, not even concern for how my sister would react to the news. I watched, glassy-eyed, while the blood-red dawn edged out the night and we drove through the back streets of Naples.

I stared at the city I had found so exciting, tears scouring my throat and making my eyes burn. Vito's face, so harsh and determined, and his hard body pressing into my softness—coaxing me to orgasm, covering me as the bullets rained above us, then thrusting me away from him as if I were garbage—were all I could see, all I could feel, as my exhausted mind tried to figure out if my night with him had even been real…

Or simply a terrifying and unbearably erotic dream.

CHAPTER SIX

Mia

Three months later

THE DAYS AND weeks which followed drifted past in a fog. But the events of that night remained vivid, coming back to me in hyper-realistic dreams.

Everything that had happened with Vito—from the moment I had first met his searing gaze on the yacht until he had thrust me away from him, the scent of blood and gunsmoke permeating my senses. I recalled every detail with startling clarity, like a movie in my mind playing on a loop, each overwhelming emotion mixed into the mêlée of images.

Vito's expression—fierce with hunger, demand and then disgust. The harsh planes and angles of his face both bad and beautiful. The helicopter ride above the city— the wind brushing my bare legs, the touch of his palm on my trembling thigh, the gush of anticipation like a drug. His callused fingers gliding over my skin, his tongue demanding my surrender, that insatiable cock driving into me. His husky voice, thick with appreciation, imagining me pregnant, his harsh plea for me to move. And the terrifying sights and sounds at dawn. The chaos, the blood, the hollow pop of gunfire something I'd never heard before and never wanted to hear again.

It all came back to me over and over again, waking me sweaty and scared each night, but also filling me with the vicious yearning which made my clitoris throb and my heart gallop.

But everything after that night and the dawn raid sank into an impenetrable fog once I had been escorted back to the UK.

The car which had left the estate had driven me to a small airfield outside Naples, where the truth had finally dawned on me.

Vito wasn't just a billionaire businessman. And he wasn't a phenomenally hot Italian aristocrat either. The secrecy, the violence which surrounded him spoke to something very different. I couldn't get my head around it though, as I struggled to keep the stress and fear and nausea from consuming me.

A private jet had been waiting for us at the airfield. I was still wrapped in the blood-stained sheet as I was escorted onto the plane and it soared into the early morning light. We landed a few hours later in another private airfield in the UK… Lorenzo had accompanied me on the plane, and once I'd managed to shake at least some of the panic and fear from my head, I asked him the questions whirring around in my tired mind.

Who was his boss really?

Why had those men been shooting at us?

Would Vito be okay?

Because even though I knew now Vito was not one of the good guys, I still couldn't get the picture out of my head of him diving across that bed to protect me. Or the bright red blood coursing down his chest from the bullet wound in his shoulder.

Lorenzo hadn't answered any of my questions, of course.

By the time we landed, I had managed to take a shower and change into some actual clothing—despite the shivers still wracking my body and the numbness in my limbs. And I'd also managed to gather at least some of my wits. Enough to know I would be better off if these men didn't know where Evie and I lived. When Lorenzo asked me for my address so the car which had arrived at the air-field could drive me home, I gave him a fake location. He stared at me for the longest time, and I had the suspicion he knew I was lying. Then he nodded and gave the fake address to the driver.

But before I could climb into the car, he grasped my arm to murmur in my ear, the veiled threat clear, 'If you speak of this night to anyone, it will be bad for you and your sister. Do you understand?'

I nodded, because I did understand. I understood totally now.

'Is Vito a mafia boss?' I asked, the words echoing in my head, and sounding impossible even as I said them.

By then, though, my mind had become foggy. I couldn't seem to feel much of anything anymore. I was living outside myself, in an alternative reality, where I'd morphed from being a teaching assistant finding her joy in Naples to a woman who had not only developed a sexual obsession with a mafia boss but had survived a shootout.

So even though I understood Vito was dangerous, I couldn't seem to get it to settle into my skull.

Lorenzo's face hardened, but he didn't look surprised

by the question. 'Don Vito is the *padrino* of the Rocco family. And he will protect what is his,' he said, the threat not even veiled anymore.

Then he nodded at the driver and let me get into the car.

The truth should have sunk in after that. The truth that I would be lucky never to see Vito again.

But my subconscious refused to play ball. It felt as if I was living my life on autopilot. Those vivid, devastating dreams which woke me up every night more real than the days I spent going through the motions of my safe but now hopelessly monochrome existence.

It wasn't that I craved Vito's attention anymore, or any man's, for that matter. I'd had my wild night, and it had left me with a trauma I was struggling to process.

It hadn't taken Evie long to get the truth out of me about Vito, even though I'd had to swear her to secrecy and get her to promise not to tell Becca or Jessie. She'd had no idea what to do about my virtually catatonic state ever since. At first, she'd searched for anything she could find out about the shootout at Vito's estate on the internet to give me closure. But there was virtually nothing, just a brief mention a week later on an Italian website about an 'incident' which may have involved a gang war in the city's western districts. But even those details were sketchy. Either the police weren't releasing any details or they didn't know what had happened either.

I waited for days for Interpol or the FBI, or the Home Office, or whoever the heck handled investigations of international crime syndicates to break down our door and interrogate me. But no one did. Which was good, because I knew I would have kept my promise not to tell them anything…not because of but *despite* Lorenzo's threat.

Didn't I owe Vito that much for saving my life?

But as the days stretched into weeks, the numbness, the nightmares—and those impossibly erotic dreams—didn't disappear. They simply morphed into exhaustion—and this weird oversensitivity in my breasts, almost as if Vito was still there, still controlling my body.

It would have freaked me out if I'd been able to care. But I was still struggling to feel anything at all until the morning Evie came down to breakfast and placed a paper bag with a pharmacy logo onto the kitchen table.

'What's that?' I asked.

She'd already suggested I go to see a doctor, or a trauma specialist—as if you'd be able to get one of those on the NHS.

'I don't need medication,' I said. 'I just need more time. I'm going to be fine.'

'You forget, I was the one who persuaded you to hook up with a man who turned out to be a bloody mafia boss, Mia. I feel responsible for nearly getting you killed. And you're not yourself. You've been weird ever since. I want to fix it.'

The guilt shadowing her eyes ripped away some of the fog. I covered her hand on the table and felt it tremble.

'Evie, don't you dare blame yourself. I was the one who made that choice…plus you weren't wrong about him giving me the night of my life,' I added, the weird urge to laugh making me wonder if I was officially losing what was left of my mind. 'And I didn't die. So it's all good. I'm starting to feel better now. Honestly, I am,' I said, trying to convince myself it was true. What scared me more than the fog, though, was the realisation I still missed Vito, especially at night, the feel of his strong body holding me and the glitter of approval in his eyes.

I hadn't lied to Evie. That one night had been the most alive I had ever felt.

Go figure.

From the sceptical look on Evie's face, she wasn't fooled. 'Maybe, but I think you need to use this now.'

I glanced at the chemist bag again. 'I'm not taking any happy pills. You know what that did to Mum…'

'I couldn't get those without a prescription, Mia,' Evie said softly, then pulled a box out of the bag and placed it in front of me. 'It's not happy pills. It's a pregnancy test.'

My mind blanked.

'It's been three months since that night,' she continued gently. 'And you've only had one light period. You're tired all the time, and your tits are enormous.'

'No way has it been that long…'

How could it have been three months? When it still felt like yesterday, because of those dreams dragging me back to Naples and Vito every single night?

The light period a week after I'd returned home had set my mind at rest about an unplanned pregnancy. So I hadn't bothered to sort out any emergency contraception. Although to be honest, I wasn't sure I would have been capable of arranging it, even without the light period, because I couldn't seem to organise much of anything anymore.

But how could I not have noticed three whole months going by?

'I know you're not always regular, so I didn't say anything. But Mia, the box with your tampons in it hasn't been touched for eight weeks.'

I stared at the test sitting in front of me. 'I can't be pregnant. It must be stress.'

Evie picked up the box, took my hand and pressed

the kit into my palm. 'Just take the test. Then we can be sure. Okay?'

I held the box as if it were an unexploded bomb. But strangely, for the first time in, well, three months, I could feel my extremities again. I wasn't numb anymore. The late July sun shining through our basement window felt bright instead of dull, my mind no longer vague. Instead, all sorts of bizarre thoughts and emotions were racing through my head in vivid Technicolor. The emotions didn't make any sense, but at least I could feel every single one of them. Panic and fear, of course, but also hope and anticipation.

Hope? Anticipation? Where were they coming from?

A pregnancy would be bad, *very* bad. What would I do if I was carrying Vito Rocco's baby?

The man who—according to the little Evie had managed to discover about him—was rumoured to run the biggest crime syndicate in southern Italy. The man who had lit up my body like a firework, saved my life and then discarded me.

The tears I hadn't shed for three months, but which had been scouring my eyeballs all this time, welled up and spilled over my lids.

Evie gripped my shoulders and gave them a soft shake. 'Don't cry, Mia. And don't panic. Until we know. Then we can figure out what to do.'

I nodded like a scared child… When exactly had my reckless baby sister become the responsible adult in this family?

We trooped up to the bathroom together. And I peed on the stick.

Five minutes later, the bottom fell out of my world

once and for all… But what replaced it wasn't numbness anymore. It was fierce, abiding love. And determination.

Because if I was going to have a mafia boss's baby, I was going to have to protect it.

I stroked my stomach, aware for the first time of the bloated feeling there. Why hadn't I noticed that either? It was pathetic.

'Will you tell him?' Evie whispered, her eyes wet, too.

I swiped the tears off my cheeks. 'I can't tell him, Evie.'

'Why? Because you're scared of him, of what he'll do…'

I shook my head. Even though I probably ought to be scared of Vito, I wasn't. Not about this.

'No, because I witnessed how dangerous his life is, and I don't want that for me or my child. He said he wanted me gone, so I'm going to give him what he wants.' Ridiculous to think it was that demand which had been the hardest to process, even after I'd finally figured out who—and what—Vito was.

Evie gripped my fingers. 'You're definitely going to have it, then?'

I nodded, knowing I didn't have a choice. I already loved the life growing inside me…because the fact of its existence had given me back my self. The fog I'd been living in since that night had cleared. That hideous sense of being outside myself. Even the guilt and recriminations which had haunted me—for being stupid enough not to question anything about that night until it was too late.

Vito could have told me who he was, but why hadn't I asked? Even his dominant, entitled behaviour which I'd found so hot, I could now see was a byproduct of who he was. A man who lived outside the law, who didn't abide by society's rules.

If anything, the wealth and power and danger surrounding Vito had intensified the adrenaline rush which had made every aspect of that night so exhilarating.

But I wasn't that clueless thrill-seeker anymore, looking to have one wild night. I would be a mother in six short months—and that gave me a purpose again. I'd once thrived on being responsible and pragmatic, on being a rule-follower. That would be my superpower now.

The strange pang in my chest I recognised from that night only plunged deeper into my chest as I realised I would never be able to see Vito again. I ignored it. Because this was my reality now. And if I was going to have a mob boss's baby, my priority had to be keeping it safe—from its father most of all.

CHAPTER SEVEN

Mia

Two months later

As I walked through the park after my first full week back at work following the long summer break, I noticed the toddlers jumping about in the water play area. Even in September, the weather was warm and sticky. The familiar wave of emotion hit me as I imagined the little boy who would be playing there too in a couple of years' time—because the sonographer had been fairly sure she'd spotted a penis during my latest scan.

I scrubbed the tears off my cheek. 'For God's sake,' I whispered.

When exactly were my emotions going to settle down? I'd never had morning sickness, but I'd had pretty much every other pregnancy symptom. Mood swings which gave me whiplash. Exhaustion which struck as soon as I got home. My boobs were officially the size of watermelons on steroids. And then there were the erotic dreams which woke me up at night, wet and swollen and so horny I had to masturbate the edge off before I could get back to sleep.

Of course, the star player in every one of those dreams had been Vito.

'*I like imagining this body pregnant with my child... It is making me want you more.*'

The words he'd said to me that night as he stroked my belly whispered across my consciousness again. I silenced the voice in my head. The torrid memories of our one night together would not help to contain the pheromone-mageddon my pregnancy had already caused.

I watched the kids while they played, instinctively cradling the compact bump where my pregnancy was starting to show. I'd bought my first pair of maternity jeans online last week—and wept all over them when they'd arrived. Because hormones. *Sheesh.*

Shouldering my bag, I carried on walking, my work shoes hurting. Being a teaching assistant meant being on my feet pretty much all day. At least today was a Friday. I could sleep all weekend if I wanted to.

Yippee.

As I turned into our road, I spotted a gleaming black SUV double-parked outside our basement flat. I stopped, the blast of memory—of the car I had been bundled into at dawn in Naples—sending shivers ricochetting down my spine and deep into my abdomen.

The hairs on my neck prickled. But then I got a grip and made myself carry on.

It was probably our upstairs neighbour Mrs Dean's son Greg come to visit. He was a very successful businessman—according to her—and he seemed incapable of ever parking properly. Of course, the last time he'd been round, he'd been driving a smaller grey SUV, but perhaps his business was so successful now he'd had an upgrade. No doubt Mrs Dean would be by tomorrow to tell us all about it.

I sighed. *Goody.*

I glanced at the car as I opened our gate, unable to see through the blacked-out windows. I picked up my pace as I hurried down the basement steps, scrambling in my purse to find my keys.

I shot inside, slammed the door behind me and leant against it, waiting for my pulse to slow. But then the phantom scent which had come to me in dreams so many times over the past five months filled my senses.

Vito's scent, the aroma of clean soap and oranges and subtle, expensive cologne.

Oh hell, was I having phantom scent delusions in the daylight now, too? *Not good.*

I swore as I dumped my bag on the hall table and kicked off my shoes. I headed to the kitchen to make myself some herbal tea and calm my shattered nerves.

But as I entered the room, I came to an abrupt halt. My thudding heartbeat rammed my chest wall. And every last molecule of blood drained from my face to surge between my thighs and make my nipples swell to attention.

'*Ciao*, Mia,' a low voice murmured, sending more shockwaves through my system.

Vito was leaning against my kitchen counter, or rather an illusion of him was. But he looked so real. He wore a white shirt rolled up to reveal those roped forearms covered with tattoos. Tailored trousers hugged his powerful thighs. His pecs bunched under the shirt as he crossed his arms over that broad chest, revealing a gun holstered under this arm. His hair was much shorter, cropped close to his head, but his face was just as I remembered it in dreams...except not. Because instead of those vivid blue eyes being dark with arousal, his features relaxed with afterglow, his stubbled jaw tightened to granite as his gaze swept to my belly.

'Vito?' I whispered, sure I had to be hallucinating. Because how could he have got in here?

Hallucinating wasn't good, but it wasn't catastrophic. Clearly the pregnancy hormones weren't through messing with me just yet. But then he spoke again, his voice hoarse with accusation, and the shock constricted around my throat.

'*Il bambino é mio, si.*' The sharp words sliced through what was left of my composure as his penetrating gaze rose to my face—the searing accusation in his eyes burning my skin.

My shattered mind started to engage.

Of course he could have got in here, Mia. The guy's a mafia don.

I didn't speak Italian, but it wasn't hard to guess what he had asked me. The lie hovered on my tongue. If I told him the baby wasn't his, would this vision disappear?

Did I want it to disappear?

Okay, what now?

Before I could even process the madness of that thought, he uncrossed his arms and marched across the kitchen. Grasping my upper arm, he carried on walking back down the hallway, hauling me with him, muttering in furious Italian, words I couldn't decipher. But when he kicked open the front door of my apartment, ready to drag me up the basement steps to the car—*his* car—my thundering heartbeat finally snapped me out of the fugue state I had entered. And reality returned in a rush.

This was real. This was happening. Vito was here, in

London, in my home. He must have broken in. And now he knew about the baby.

I grabbed the door frame as he hauled me through it, gripping hard enough to make my fingernails scrape the wood. I couldn't let him get me out of the flat and put me in that car.

I had no idea what he was thinking. Or where he was planning to take me. Had I seen the flicker of shock in his eyes before he'd masked it? I didn't know, because he'd turned into the all-powerful and furious mob boss so fast. But one thing was for sure. The seductive man who had got off on the idea of seeing me pregnant was long gone now. Perhaps he had never even existed.

'Let go,' he growled, the fury in his voice unmistakable.

I shook my head, tightening my death grip. 'If you try to take me anywhere, I'll scream my lungs out!' I said, sounding surprisingly calm considering a mafia boss had broken into my flat and was in the process of kidnapping me.

He banded one muscular forearm around my waist, above the baby bump, and leaned close. 'If you do this, Mia,' he growled against my ear, sending traitorous shivers down my neck, 'I will gag you.'

Before I could respond to the threat, he gave a sharp tug, yanking my fingers free of the door frame. I was so shocked at how easily he was manhandling me, I was mute as he hefted me up the basement steps. But when we got to the top and I found my feet, I filled my lungs, preparing to scream.

Before a single sound could come out, though, a large hand covered my mouth, choking off my attempt to alert everyone within a ten-mile radius.

I bit down as hard as I could, but despite the hiss of pain from behind me, his hand remained firmly in place.

He swore again in Italian as Lorenzo and another man appeared in front of us, ready to assist their boss in subduing me. As he spoke to them in low, staccato sentences, I tried to sink my teeth into his hand, but his palm was clamped so tight over my mouth, I couldn't get enough purchase.

I probably should have been terrified. But instead I was furious. Tears of anger and determination leaked out of my eyes as I struggled against his iron-hard hold. He wasn't hurting me, but I felt completely controlled by his big body, unable to move, unable to speak. I kicked at his shins, but without any shoes on, the soft thuds were probably hurting me more than him. Meanwhile Lorenzo—the bastard—produced a red silk sash and a couple of zip ties from his jacket pocket.

I began to struggle even harder. What the hell? Did they carry kidnap equipment around with them?

'Stop. You will hurt yourself and the babe,' Vito demanded.

You're the one that's doing that!

I yelled my reply into his hand, but it came out in a series of garbled grunts.

He lifted his hand, and I had just enough time to suck in a breath—ready to empty my lungs in a scream I hoped would be audible in Scotland Yard five miles away—when the silk was banded across my mouth, forcing my jaw open. Within seconds it had been secured behind my head. Panic joined my fury as I struggled to dislodge it with my tongue without any success. Had he done this before? He seemed to be an expert.

'If you behave,' he said, his tone cold, 'I will not tie your hands and feet.'

More muffled grunts came from me.

Where was everyone? He was doing this in broad daylight. I had some vague idea if I could just delay him from putting me in the car, everything would be okay. Surely someone would alert the police. But as I continued to struggle against his hold, banging my heels against his shins, he tugged my arms behind my back and used a zip tie on my wrists while Lorenzo knelt down to secure my ankles.

Within seconds, I was trussed up like a chicken. He scooped me into his arms. I wriggled furiously as another bodyguard whipped open the SUV's passenger door. Vito climbed into the back of the vehicle and settled me on his lap. I was sweaty and breathless, and so furious I was practically seeing stars.

How could he do this to me against my will? And why?

The car door slammed, and Lorenzo and the other guard climbed into the front seats. Suddenly we were speeding out of my road and through the streets of Ealing. In minutes the car had turned onto the busy road that led out of London.

Vito held me securely, stifling my struggles, almost as if he was cradling me in his arms. I whipped my head back in one last desperate attempt to hurt him, but he simply lifted his chin out of my line of fire. Then he clasped my jaw and forced my gaze to meet his.

'Stop, now, or you will remain tied for the whole flight. Do you understand?'

Flight? What flight? Was he planning to take me out of the country?

I blinked furiously, tugging against the bonds on my

hands, the zip ties digging into my wrists, the fury giving way to mindless panic.

I shook my head furiously. But it was futile and frustrating, the silk gag making my words unintelligible.

His jaw remained tight—the muscle in it ticking ominously. But otherwise he looked completely unmoved.

Finally, I stopped struggling, because what was the point? He obviously had no regrets about what he'd done. And I had to conserve my energy to figure out how to escape him. *Somehow.* And get word to Evie.

God, Evie.

The panic blindsided me, making my breathing hit warp speed and my chest feel as if someone had dropped a boulder on it.

My sister would come home to find me gone—without a trace. I didn't even have my purse with me. She'd be beside herself with worry.

I shook my head again, pleading with my eyes now. He had to let me go.

'Do not be afraid. I will not hurt you,' he said, even though he already had. He'd invaded my home and kidnapped me!

But then his gaze dropped to my bump, and he covered it with his palm. His hand felt warm through the cotton of my dress as he smoothed the fabric over my rounded belly. I spotted the teeth marks on the web of skin between his thumb and forefinger. The livid red dots stood out against the tattoo of a serpent which snaked down his wrist.

I hope that hurts, I thought miserably.

But then his roaming palm rose to cradle my breast. I shuddered, the jolt of desire shocking and unstoppable as he brushed the rigid nipple through my clothing as if testing its responsiveness, the fascination on his face clear.

'Your breasts are even more glorious now that your body is ripe with my child,' he said, his tone fierce with possessiveness. 'Your nipples already beg for my mouth.'

I shook my head again—trying to deny it, even though my breasts felt swollen and heavy under his caresses, the nipple engorged in response to his touch.

Humiliation engulfed me. I didn't want him to caress me like a lover. Except my body was calling me a liar, the hot boulder wedged between my thighs reminding me how good it had felt to have him buried inside me.

He pressed his lips to my sweaty hair and let out a rough laugh—the cynical edge sharpened by the dark craving in his eyes.

'You are a wild cat, Mia.' He shook his hand and sucked on the raw skin where I'd bit him. 'I may need a tetanus shot.' He chuckled as if my attempts to free myself were amusing. *Damn him.* 'You should have told me of the baby.' His features hardened into that brooding mask. 'But you are mine now, and I will protect you both. How easy or hard you make that for yourself is up to you.'

The words sounded like a promise as much as a threat. The tears I'd been trying so hard not to shed leaked out. He brushed his thumb across my cheek, the tender gesture as unsettling as it was disconcerting.

I swung my head away from him, the only act of defiance left to me, my breathing ragged with emotion. Slipping a small penknife out of his pocket, he flipped it open with one hand and reached behind me to cut the tie digging into my wrists. Dragging my hands into my lap, he rubbed the reddened skin.

I probably ought to have used the opportunity to pull off the gag, but I didn't. Because I had nothing to say to him. What *could* I say that would get through to him?

He'd obviously spent his whole life doing whatever the hell he wanted. But then he tugged the gag down himself.

'You should not have struggled,' he said, his gaze fixed on the raw skin as he soothed it with his thumbs. Was that regret I could hear in his voice?

'Well, maybe you shouldn't have kidnapped me,' I said, unable to keep the anger out of my voice.

I didn't care if he was the most powerful mafioso in Italy. He was way out of line.

'I am not kidnapping you. I am protecting you,' he announced, the righteous, dictatorial tone back.

Yeah, definitely not regret then.

'I don't want or need your protection,' I announced. 'Especially when it involves me being tied up and gagged…' I replied, more determined now than ever to stand up to him.

I'd been clueless once, and starry-eyed about this man, so pathetically grateful for his attention I'd let myself be used. But I wasn't clueless anymore.

I probably ought to be scared of him. He didn't respect boundaries of any kind. Somehow, though, I knew he wouldn't hurt me, not physically. What he clearly didn't get, though, was that taking all my choices away from me was another way of hurting me, which was far worse in many ways. I'd been here before with my mother, and it sucked.

His dark brows lowered. The flinty look he sent me was filled with frustration rather than anger—as if I was an annoying thorn in his side which he did not understand.

'If you had done as you were told, the ties and the gag would not have been necessary,' he said, missing the point completely.

I scoffed. 'Stop gaslighting me.'

He frowned. 'Gaslighting? What does this mean?'

'It means what you just did…' I glared at him. 'Suggesting it was my fault those ties cut into my wrists when you had no right to put them on me in the first place.'

He didn't look convinced. 'You did not do as I demanded,' he said, still gaslighting me. 'So I had every right.'

'Uh-huh, and who made you the boss of me, exactly?'

His eyes widened a fraction, signalling his surprise at my defiance. But then he rested his hand on my abdomen again, caressing the spot where our baby grew—the sense of entitlement beyond shocking. I gasped as an arrow of heat plunged into my sex. His voice had lowered to a husky growl when he spoke. 'I am the boss of many people, Mia. But *you* most of all, now that you carry my child.'

'Just because I'm pregnant doesn't mean you own me…' I said, my voice shaky as I shoved his hand away.

'Your body does not agree,' he said, clasping my head. His lips hovered over mine—the intent to kiss me if I gave him any encouragement.

I flattened my palms against his chest, which felt like a slab of marble, determined to push him away. The last thing I needed right now was to reignite the passion which had got me into this situation in the first place.

But instead of forcing the connection, instead of grinding his mouth against mine, he licked the seam, coaxing me to accept his dominance. And succumb to the desire already burning through my bloodstream. His thumb caressed my neck where my pulse thundered, even as he held me still.

'Open for me, Mia,' he murmured against my quivering lips.

I could smell him, that intoxicating scent of soap and man. The melting sensation throbbed and pulsed between my thighs, reawakening all those erotic dreams which had plagued me for the past five months. The fire inside me ignited like a firecracker, making my breasts swell and my panties dampen. I writhed against his hold, but my mouth opened on a sob of surrender, my body needing this, as my determination to resist my reaction to his demands shattered. He thrust his tongue deep, possessing my mouth in greedy, searing, seductive strokes, angling my head to take more. The kiss became carnal, basic, elemental, our physical connection even stronger now than it had been before.

Fighting the yearning at the taste of him again after so long was impossible, my body primed by my pregnancy to do whatever he demanded. Our tongues danced, tangled, my fingers curling into his shirt to drag him closer, my bottom shifting on his lap, desperate to feel the thick ridge I was sitting on inside me again.

He dragged his mouth away first, leaving me panting with need. But as he stroked my hair back from my face, his gaze dark with knowledge and no small degree of satisfaction at my instant and incendiary response to him, I jerked my head away from his touch. And released my death grip on his shirt.

'It doesn't prove anything…' I managed, but I could hear my own defensiveness. And knew he could hear it too, when a smug smile lifted his lips and embarrassment joined the sting of beard burn on my cheeks. 'Just because you can make me respond to you does not mean I belong to you.'

'Does it not?' he said, the self-satisfaction in his tone even more galling than the melting sensation in my panties.

Who was I kidding? He'd devoured me, and I'd encouraged him. Even now I could feel the outline of his erection prodding me. And instead of disgusting me, it was making me hot.

Really, Mia? How can you still want him when he's just kidnapped you?

I struggled against his hold, desperate to get off his lap now before I lost the last of my dignity. And self-respect. Or he took even more advantage of my inability to resist him.

'Sit still,' he said, his voice strained, as he wrapped his arms around me, holding me in place. 'Or I may be forced to prove my point in front of my men.'

Apparently he was as close to the edge as I was, which could have been some consolation but wasn't. Because if he chose to take me in the car, I wasn't entirely sure I had the willpower to stop him.

The car accelerated onto the motorway, and his arms tightened on my aching body.

'*Dormi*, bella,' he murmured against my hair as he placed his hand onto my head and pressed my cheek to his shirt. 'We will continue this discussion when you are safe.'

I didn't know what *dormi* meant, but I could guess, the exhaustion settling around me like a cloud.

But I gathered the last of my energy and dragged my head free of his hold to send him the hardest stare I could muster.

'I'm not sleeping on your lap.' I couldn't fight him physically. He was much stronger than I was. And apparently, I couldn't even resist his kisses. But I refused to let him treat me like a lover. I was here against my will, whether I had responded to that damn kiss or not, and he needed to be reminded of that.

Something akin to astonishment flickered in his eyes.

Again with the surprise... Was he really that used to people, especially women, just obeying his every command without question?

He frowned, not pleased with my resistance.

But it was my turn to be surprised when he lifted me off his lap. It was impossible to sit properly on the leather seat with my ankles still bound. I had to do something about that if I was going to have any chance of escaping him.

With that in mind, I said as nonchalantly as I could, 'Can you free my legs? The tie is starting to cut into my ankles, and I can't get comfortable.'

His eyes narrowed. 'I will cut you loose if I have your word you will not run from me again, Mia.'

Yeah, right.

My temper spiked. But I bit down on the contemptuous comeback. Talking back to him before had only earned me that devastating kiss.

'You have my word, Vito,' I said with all the conviction I could muster while lying through my teeth. What right did he have to demand my obedience? Apart from the gun holstered under his arm.

He wasn't going to shoot me, though. I knew that much. Because I was carrying his child.

But did he really feel some kind of connection to the baby, or was his reaction to my pregnancy just a part of his conviction that both of us now belonged to him?

How could it be more than that when he didn't care

about my feelings, and when he'd had no qualms about stealing us from our home?

I would have been safer in London, living anonymously, than I could ever be with him. I'd watched him get shot less than six months ago. I'd even been shot at myself that night.

The memories I'd worked so hard to suppress resurfaced as he leant across me to lift my feet into his lap and slice through the zip tie with his knife. He stroked my ankles, soothing the sore skin. I jerked my feet free, not appreciating the tingling sensations sprinting up my legs from his touch. He raised an eyebrow at my defiance—but when he shrugged, his features tightened. He rolled his shoulder as he straightened.

And the memories flooded back again. The acrid scent of gunsmoke, the metallic smell of blood. *His* blood.

'Is your shoulder, okay?' The question popped out before I could prevent it.

He glanced at me, apparently surprised by the question. I'd surprised myself by asking it. By even caring about the answer. But I couldn't seem to stop myself from nodding towards the shoulder he'd rolled, the one he'd been shot in, as I put on my seat belt.

'Your right shoulder. Is it fully healed?' I added, feeling foolish now, especially when the wave of gratitude returned as I remembered how he had thrown himself across my body to shield me from harm.

It doesn't make him a hero, Mia. Or you beholden to him. If he'd mentioned he was a mafia don, you wouldn't even have been in his bed to get shot at in the first place.

Of course, that meant I also wouldn't have the baby growing inside me, which I loved already. But my pregnancy had been an accident. The ambush that night certainly hadn't been. It was a by-product of the dangerous life he led that I wanted no part of.

He massaged the shoulder muscle absently. 'It is sometimes stiff, nothing more. It was only a scratch,' he said, dropping his hand. 'I have had worse.'

I couldn't hide my shock at his nonchalance. Was he being macho about the wound, or did he *really* not consider it to be that significant?

I knew his injury that night hadn't been a scratch. There had been enough blood to soak through the sheet. It made me think of the many other scars I'd noticed on his body which I'd found so hot that night…

Those scars were a lot less sexy now. As I wondered how many other wounds he'd sustained, and how bad they must have been for him to be so indifferent about this one… I swallowed to control the well of sympathy making my throat raw.

Stop feeling sorry for him. He chose this life.

All his answer really told me was that he was as reckless and cavalier with his own safety as he was currently being with mine.

Flicking the knife closed, he stuffed it back into his pants pocket. 'You should sleep. We have a long journey ahead of us before we reach Isla Donna.'

The panic returned, tightening around my already raw throat. So he *was* planning to take me out of the country.

'Where is that?' I said, attempting to calm my breathing and control my thundering heartbeats.

I couldn't let him get me on a plane. I would have to find a way to run, especially now he'd untied my legs. I had to believe that, or I would freak out completely.

'It is an island I own in the Bay of Naples. It is where you will be safe. And where my baby will be born,' he murmured, his voice becoming huskier as his gaze drifted to my bump again. His gaze hardened with an iron will when it rose back to my face. The harsh expression was both fiercely possessive and dark with an awareness which made a blush flame across my collarbones and rise up my neck.

I nodded, knowing I couldn't speak, while the sexual charge which was always there between us—and had intensified since my pregnancy—crackled over my skin like wildfire again from that one incendiary look. Because then he would know how easily he could trigger my arousal, if he didn't already. And that would be bad.

I didn't belong to him, even though my body reacted to him, and neither did this baby.

But the riot of sensations he had triggered with that one hot look had the exhaustion settling over me like a heavy blanket. My mouth cracked open in a huge yawn.

He clasped my neck, the calluses strangely comforting as well as annoyingly arousing as he brushed my cheek with his thumb. '*Dormi*, Mia. And when you are safe, I will give you all the orgasms you need.'

Orgasms? What?

I lurched back. 'I don't need any more orgasms from you,' I managed. But what should have been a slap down instead sounded like a come-on, because my voice had dropped several octaves, too.

The knowing smile he sent me only made his handsome face look more gorgeous. *The bastard.* 'I can smell that is a lie,' he said with a self-satisfied chuckle.

I turned away to stare out of the window, deciding I was way too shattered right now to argue with him—and his gargantuan ego. I had a lot of planning to do before we reached the airfield. Annoyingly, though, I could smell what he could smell—the rich, sultry scent as my panties dampened with need.

Terrific.

I stared at my reflection in the dark glass, the motorway lights blurring as we drove to who knew where, and I struggled to figure out an escape plan.

Perhaps I could steal his knife, or even his gun. I shivered in the warm car.

I'd never touched a gun before in my life, and I had no idea how to use one.

I blinked, determined to keep my eyes open and focus.

But my body felt so heavy, as if I'd been through a war. Probably because I had.

I was in a state of shock, which had lowered my ability to resist the physical pull of the man beside me, who was now talking into his mobile in Italian, having forgotten all about me.

Exhaustion and anxiety and frustration. That's why I'd succumbed to his damn kiss—and why I felt as if I had a hot rock wedged between my thighs, which was throbbing in time with my heart beats. And why my limbs felt as if they weighed a thousand tons, and why formulating a viable escape plan seemed more insurmountable right now than attempting to free solo El Capitan with my ankles still zip-tied together.

I blinked slowly.

I yawned again and rested my forehead on the glass. I watched the lights of the other cars heading out of London on a Friday night, mesmerised by the streams blending with the red glow of the approaching dusk on the horizon.

Don't fall asleep, Mia. Don't you dare. You're the only one who can rescue you. But you have to stay awake...

I kept repeating the mantra in my head even as the

quite hum of the car's powerful engine, the low timbre of Vito's voice talking in Italian and the motorway lights cocooned me in the comforting black.

CHAPTER EIGHT

Vito

'Do you wish me to carry her to the plane, *padrino*?' Lorenzo murmured softly in Italian through the car's partition.

I shook my head, my gaze fixed on the woman beside me as the car stopped in the airport hangar, where my private jet stood fuelled and waiting to fly us back to Naples. From there we could travel by helicopter to Isla Donna.

'No, I will do that.' *Because no man touches her but me.*

I did not voice the thought. Lorenzo did not require an explanation to obey me. Unlike the woman who had consumed my thoughts for months now. Ever since I had recovered from the gunshot wound which had nearly killed me.

I had lied to Mia about the severity of the injury. It *should* have been no more than a scratch. But fighting off Dante and the small army he had brought with him that night had taken precedent over everything else. As a result, I had lost more blood than I could afford to lose by the time I had received medical attention. Add to that an infection which had lasted weeks, and my recovery, once we had secured the estate, had been frustratingly slow.

Dante had gone to ground now, but once he reappeared, I would kill him. What other choice had he left me—now he had challenged my rule of the Rocco empire so openly? When Dante had chosen to attack us, the feelings I had for that boy, my half brother—who had once followed me around like an eager puppy, before our father discarded him so brutally—had died.

But as I had lain in seclusion on Isla Donna, my body wracked by fever, directing the business from my sickbed while my consigliere kept news of my condition secret—feeling weaker than I had as a boy after a beating from my stepfather—my mind had drifted too many times to the other events of that night, before the bullets had started to fly.

Lorenzo had got Mia out of Italy before anyone had identified her as I had ordered him to do… Seeing her so vulnerable, terrified and naked in my bed as the bullets rained around us, missing her by millimetres, had affected me in a way I had not expected. Violence and death were a hazard of my profession which I had accepted long ago—not just for myself, but for anyone connected to me. Except I had not been so accepting that night with her… Which was why I had been determined never to see her again. She was artless, innocent, a tourist, with no clue who I was. And no understanding of the omertà that bound my family and my men.

But why then had I been unable to forget her? She was just another of the many, *many* women who had warmed my bed. Perhaps it was the delirium, the night sweats which I had endured in the early weeks after the gun battle. Or even those titanic orgasms—our insane chemistry, the scent of her arousal haunting my dreams and waking me heavy with need. Even my doctor had commented on the fact that in the throes of the fever I had mumbled her name, while my cock remained impressively hard.

The man had thought it a sign of my virility. Me, not so much.

Even after four long months, when I was finally recovered enough to resume full control of the Rocco Syndicate and begin hunting down Dante and his men, I continued to dream of her, constantly, forced to take myself in hand most nights to fall into a fitful sleep.

Eventually I had conceded Mia was a distraction I could not afford. Losing focus was dangerous to me and my men—not to mention my business interests. But the only way to free myself from this obsession was to get her out of my system.

Our one night had been cut short too soon, that was all. I still had the sultry taste of her on my tongue. I still yearned to feel her clenching around my cock. Once I had ridden her hard and long, the hold she had over me would be gone. Only then would I be free of this addiction, free to concentrate again on the only thing that mattered in my life—ensuring the empire I controlled continued to thrive, and I put an end to any threat from my half brother.

So I had arranged a clandestine flight to London to see her one last time.

But of course, when she walked into her kitchen, and I saw her condition, the damn obsession had become turbocharged. Mia had taken a piece of me with her. A piece which I would never knowingly abandon. Any more than I could now abandon her.

As the mother of my child, she would be a target. That she had not contacted me and told me of the pregnancy—

and demanded my protection—infuriated me. Her resistance had left me with no choice but to bind her wrists and ankles. I had not intended to hurt her—but the sight of her raw skin had triggered something I had buried a long time ago…the brutal image of my mother bruised and bleeding, her eyes tired, her spirit broken, just before she had taken her own life.

My gaze drifted over the mound of Mia's belly, and those full breasts. The spike of lust, the brutal blow of memory and the possessive fury tangled into a knot in my stomach. I decided once we were on Isla Donna, I must make Mia submit to me, to force her to accept I controlled her future now. Any threats against me could threaten her now too, and our child—and I would not allow her naïveté to put either herself or the baby in jeopardy.

I climbed out of the car, spoke briefly to Lorenzo— instructing him to inform the pilot not to initiate take off until our passenger was secured aboard the plane—and walked around the car to open Mia's door. Then the hollow ache appeared in my chest. The ache from my childhood which I had destroyed, until that night in Naples when Mia had been shot at. The ache I hated, because it made me feel weak, made me feel like that broken boy again who had been unable to protect his own mother.

I would have to destroy that ache. But Mia was mine now—the fierce attraction between us even stronger and more intense than ever.

Eventually I would tire of her, because no woman had ever held my attention for long. But until that happened, I would exploit that attraction.

I unstrapped her seat belt and lifted her as gently as I could so as not to wake her. My arms tightened around her as I strode to the jet.

She sighed and snuggled into my chest, her body becoming limp and pliant. The tidal wave of lust was joined by the swift wave of protectiveness.

It is only because she carries your child.

It meant nothing, I decided. I was not a soft man, given to sentimental emotions. But even so, I found myself cradling her as I climbed the plane steps and walked to the bedroom at the back. I placed her on the bed. She rolled over, her knees rising to her chest as if she were protecting our child—*my* child. The hollow ache expanded as I noticed the marks on her wrists caused by the bindings when she tucked her hands under her cheek.

'You should not have defied me, Mia,' I murmured.

I grabbed a couple of silk ties from the wardrobe of suits I kept on the plane and returned to the bed. Holding her bare foot, I wrapped the silk around her ankle and secured it to the bed. Then I took the other tie and secured one hand as loosely as I could to the top of the frame.

I stared at her, lying there bound to my bed. But as well as the familiar heat, was the sense of something lost. I shook off the unfamiliar feeling of regret.

She must accept my dominance—just like everyone who had sworn allegiance to me. By going through with the pregnancy, she had made that choice.

I walked out of the cabin and locked the door. If she started to yell, no one would listen. And she would not be able to hurt herself secured to the bed.

She would be mad when she woke. But there would be time enough to address her attitude problem once we arrived on Isla Donna.

Desire surged into my cock at the thought of the battles ahead.

But as my body heated, I forced the coldness into my

heart to destroy that hollow ache. The same coldness which had kept me alive as a boy and eventually made me as ruthless and successful as my father. My true father, Don Salvatore Rocco.

The man my mother had thought she was saving me from when she had run from the Rocco family. Just as Mia had attempted to do when she kept her pregnancy a secret from me. I let my anger at that decision return to destroy the pointless regret.

My father had been my salvation. Just as I would be my child's.

I owed it to Salvatore Rocco and to my legacy—not to mention that beaten, terrified boy—never to allow what was mine to be threatened.

And that included Mia now. And our baby, whether she liked it or not.

I would be the victor. Because unlike my father, I would never make the mistake he had—of trusting anyone too much, least of all a woman.

And certainly not a woman who had already betrayed me once by not informing me she carried my child.

CHAPTER NINE

Mia

'HMM.' I SIGHED, my body clumsy with sleep, my mind drifting on a sea of relaxation. But as I stretched to relieve the kink in my shoulder, my wrist snagged on something, and I couldn't lower my arm.

I opened my eyes, reality beckoning me. Suddenly Vito wasn't a hot erotic dream anymore but a disturbing memory—tying my arms and legs, sitting me on his lap and kissing me into submission.

Then I became aware of the engine noise and the night sky visible through the plane window next to the bed I was lying on.

I was on the plane. His plane. *No, no, no.*

I lurched upright, only to be jerked back onto the satin bedspread. I struggled to get into a sitting position again, but I couldn't raise my left hand—or my right knee.

Then I spotted the silk wrapped around my ankle.

What. The. Actual. Hell! He's tied me up again.

Far worse, though, was the realisation I had missed my window of opportunity to escape him in England.

Mia, you idiot. You fell asleep. And let him get you on the damn plane.

My head dropped back on the bed. I used my other hand to cradle the baby growing in my womb. And tried to calm my breathing.

Tears of anger and frustration leaked out of my eyes to trickle down the side of my face. I brushed them away with my free hand. I couldn't give him the satisfaction of seeing me cry.

But this was bad. Very bad. How was I going to escape him now?

At least I didn't feel exhausted anymore. I decided not to think about how ironic it was I'd slept so well while bound to his bed.

I had no idea what he intended to do with me. But given his line of work and the fact he'd had no compunction about kidnapping me and flying me out of the UK, I had to accept how ruthless he was. And how hard it was going to be to get away from him.

No one knew where I was. Even if Evie figured out my disappearance was Vito's doing, she would have no idea where he'd taken me. And she could hardly go to the authorities when we had both said nothing for over five months about my night with a mafioso and the baby I was carrying.

I reached above my head with my free hand and plucked at the knotted silk on my wrist, determined to at least get off his bed.

I had broken a nail and was huffing and puffing with frustration five minutes later, still attempting to untie the knot—because Vito had clearly been a bloody Boy Scout in another life—when a swooping sensation in my stomach signalled the plane was losing altitude.

Were we landing already? How long had I been asleep?

Then the cabin door opened. I shifted round on the bed

and glared at the tall figure who strolled into the room without an invitation.

'You are awake, Mia.' Vito's casual greeting had my indignation snapping to attention. 'I hope you slept well.'

'Of course I didn't. How could I when you tied me to the bed?' I snapped, even though it wasn't true. 'You have to untie me,' I added, hating the plea in my voice.

He frowned as if my demand was anathema to him. 'There is nothing I *have* to do where you are concerned,' he said, the arrogance I hated back full force. 'You are mine now, Mia. It is time you accepted this.'

'I'll never accept it,' I shot back, determined to fight his dominance.

'Do you wish me to prove it?' he replied, sitting on the bed.

'No…' I said, but when I attempted to kick him with my free foot, he caught my ankle and held my leg down easily.

'Stop this or you will force my hand,' he murmured as his thumb caressed the inside of my ankle and made the swooping sensation in my stomach worse.

'Let go of me,' I demanded, but my attempts to jerk my foot out of his hold were to no avail. 'And stop touching me. I don't like it…' I said, desperate for him to stop that stroking motion, because the prickles of sensation I recognised all too well were shooting straight into my sex. Triggering the yearning I couldn't control even now.

I had loved his dominance that night, the chance to forget all my responsibilities and let him take control… That my body was still enthralled by him felt like a betrayal now, though.

'I can already smell this is a lie, Mia,' he said as he kept me pinned to the bed, his free hand travelling up my leg.

'What are you doing?' I gasped as the prickles went bananas and my thighs quivered, the heat pounding so hard in my sex now that the scent of my arousal was thick in the air.

'Proving how much you enjoy this,' he murmured, the seductive tone—and the sure, entitled, dominating caress—sapping my strength and my resistance.

'I… P-please…' I said, but I wasn't even sure what I was begging him for anymore as his callused palm continued its ascent—stroking my calf, then brushing the inside of my thigh. My struggles died, my pleas for him to stop turning to a moan of encouragement as his marauding hand disappeared under my dress and his thumb caressed the seam of skin between my leg and my torso.

I trembled violently, my back arching, my clit already desperate for his touch, his thumb tantalisingly close to the lace barrier already damp with need.

'*Bella ragazza*,' he murmured, his voice husky with need too. The dark demand in his eyes was my undoing.

Releasing my ankle, because all the fight had gone out of me, he flipped up my dress to expose my panties. He clasped my thighs to spread my legs, then climbed onto the bed, positioning himself between my knees, then leant down to blow across the damp lace covering my needy clitoris.

'Y-yes…' I moaned, my desire to fight his control over my body washed away on a wave of desperation. I needed this release. The release only he had ever given me. Just once more.

Using that devious thumb, he inched the lace aside, baring my sex to his gaze.

'You are so wet and swollen for me, Mia,' he murmured, the whisper of his breath against my slick folds almost more than I could bear. 'And that scent. I must taste you.'

I writhed against his hold again, but this time to get closer, to have him put his mouth on me again. 'Then do it,' I begged.

'Promise to obey me, Mia, and I will give you what you need.'

'I—I can't…' I cried, even as I could feel what was left of my willpower dissolving. 'You shouldn't have kidnapped me.'

'And you should not have kept your pregnancy from me…' he countered, his tone sharp, his stark expression matching the clash of emotions inside me. Desperation, anger, but also desire, need, and that strange tug of hope.

'I—I had to,' I murmured, willing him to understand. 'Your life is so dangerous. I—I didn't want my baby hurt.'

He frowned, but instead of acknowledging my fears, he licked across my folds, his rough tongue lathing the aching bud. The raw sensation was like a firecracker lighting me from within, but he stopped almost instantly, leaving me teetering on the verge of a merciless orgasm. Too far gone and yet not able to tip over into the abyss.

'The only way to keep *our* baby safe is to submit to me, Mia,' he demanded, his tone harsh, but his gaze was shadowed with something much more disturbing.

Was that tenderness? Regret? How could it be, when he refused to give me a choice?

'I—I won't…' I said.

I'd been helpless once before. My desire-drenched brain could grasp that much, at least. During all the years of my childhood, my mother had put her search for the next high, the next deadbeat boyfriend, the next good time above me and Evie.

I'd learned young never to rely on anyone. I couldn't surrender that. Especially not to a man as dangerous and dictatorial as Vito. No matter how many orgasms he could give me.

'Yes, you will,' he demanded, his voice harsh. 'You must.'

But before I could reply, he delved again with his tongue, circling that aching spot and making me buck against his hold. A moan of raw, unrequited need broke free from my lips. I writhed beneath him, becoming delirious, trying to lift into his mouth, desperate for that denied release.

'It is the only way to keep you safe,' he demanded.

I wanted to tell him no… I could never submit my independence, my freedom, nor could I accept his total dominance of my life, no matter how much I enjoyed his dominance in bed…

But before I could enunciate any of it, he nudged the hood of my clit back, fastened his lips on the swollen nub and sucked.

The pleasure exploded in raw, shocking, overpowering waves that launched me off the bed, my sobs turning to groans as the orgasm crested.

Afterglow drenched me, but he continued to suckle. The tortured nub became unbearably tender as another wave of raw pleasure blasted through me.

At last he lifted his head, and I collapsed onto the bed. I could see my juices surrounding his mouth, the sight intensely erotic as he licked his lips.

'You will submit,' he murmured again. 'I will make you.'

I lay shaking, shivering, sated, but also hideously exposed, because it felt as if he had robbed a part of my soul. I *had* submitted. I *had* surrendered to him again.

But when he stood abruptly, I saw the outline of his erection jutting obscenely to tent his suit pants. My sex clenched and released, wanting to feel that huge length inside me once more.

Instead of unzipping himself, though, he tugged my panties back into place, then dragged my dress down. He lifted my chin with his thumb and forefinger, forcing my gaze to his.

'You will not escape from me. I will protect my child, no matter what you want,' he murmured.

The threat was clear, his expression deliberately blank, as he demonstrated his control over me. But when he untied my ankle and my wrist, I could see the tension in his jaw, feel the tremor in his fingers. And I knew he was not as composed or as in control as he was making out.

He could not hide his hunger for me, any more than I could hide my hunger for him. And somehow that felt important… Although I would have to wait until the endorphins had stopped charging around my system, and my brain had a chance to engage again, before I could figure out *why* it was important.

Right now, I was just a mass of throbbing sensations and aching vulnerabilities. Forced to accept that however bad a man he was, my body was totally and utterly addicted to him.

'Strap yourself in for landing,' he murmured, indicating the seat at the side of the cabin, then turned to leave.

I sat up, uncomfortably aware of the tender spot he had exploited so skilfully still throbbing incessantly between my legs.

'I w-won't submit…' I said again, knowing I had to

believe it, or I would lose what little freedom I had left. 'No matter how many times you seduce me.'

He glanced over his shoulder, his eyes flinty with temper. I don't know why I found that more encouraging than the controlled expression of moments before, but I did.

'Do not test me, Mia. I have all the power here, and you none. Remember that.'

The threat echoed in the room as he slammed the cabin door behind him and I heard the lock click. But weirdly the show of strength, the flash of temper felt like progress—despite the realisation he wasn't wrong about the massive power imbalance between us.

I flopped back on the bed, my head racing along with my heart. But while I had been ashamed of how easily I had succumbed before in the car, I didn't feel ashamed anymore.

We had a raw, elemental physical connection—something I'd never experienced before. And I *had* chosen to have his baby knowing who he was, so I needed to own that decision now.

Even though he had behaved abominably by stealing me from my home, I sensed he was much more conflicted than he wanted to be. Perhaps that was just wishful thinking on my part. But I had to find the chink in his armour, if there was one…

Please let there be a chink.

But how?

Challenging him and his view of me as someone he could make submit to his will was the only way forward now. Because escaping from him—from this whole situation—was next to impossible without his help. Perhaps it had been doomed from the start. His determination to not only claim his child but protect it was something I had not expected, when I should have.

I'd always considered myself pragmatic and practical and smart. To discover I had a side of me that wanted the thrills Vito could offer me was scary enough. But far worse would be giving him control of my safety and security—a man who was about as far as it was possible to get from safe and secure.

But attempting to fight this attraction was a lost cause, because every time he touched me, I responded.

I had to figure out how to make him see me as more than someone to be manipulated and owned. The only problem was, I didn't know anything about him, other than that he could be totally ruthless...

Perhaps the baby was the key. And understanding whether he had a genuine connection to it, or the baby was just another thing he now considered he owned... like he felt he owned me.

This could just be another power trip for a man who already held all the power in this relationship. Somehow or other I was going to have to find a way to get some power back. And the only hold I seemed to have over him was his hunger for me... Unfortunately, I had absolutely no idea how to use that to my advantage the way he could so effortlessly.

Vito

As I slammed the cabin door and snapped the lock, I was furious.

My cock throbbed—so engorged it felt as if the slightest touch would send me over. The sight of her eyes, round in her expressive face as she'd stared at me, the dark desire in the mossy green telling me she wanted me too, had nearly undone me completely.

How could I control this situation if I could not control myself? I had never been so on edge before, never undone by a woman. But the mound of her pregnancy, the feel of her lush flesh quivering with want as I stroked her thighs, those raw cries as I had licked her to climax.

Dio, I could feast on those sounds, that taste, for the rest of my life. Even though she had done the worst thing she could do to me…tried to keep my child a secret from me. The way my mother had done to my father by running from him as soon as she discovered herself pregnant— and then never finding the courage to escape from the man who had made both our lives a misery.

Had Mia known how close I was to burying myself inside her again?

I raked my fingers through my hair and strapped myself in for the plane's nighttime descent into the secret airfield I owned on the outskirts of Naples.

Surely my loss of control was just another manifestation of our extraordinary chemistry. Because there was no doubt seeing her slender body round with my baby felt as if I had branded her as mine in the most elemental way possible—and her refusal to accept that, no matter how much she wanted me, had left me feeling raw and angry.

The plane banked over the city, descended towards the airfield, then landed and taxied to a stop. After unsnapping my belt, I strode to the front of the plane and charged down the steps. My men were already gathered, guarding the runway's perimeter, a line of SUVs waiting to transport us to the heliport at the Naples estate. But I had other business to attend to first. Business I had arranged as soon as the plane had left London.

Lorenzo approached.

'Is the obstetrician waiting?' I asked without preamble.

He nodded. '*Si, padrino.* He has been paid an exorbitant sum as you requested to open his surgery tonight. But Gattuso thinks it is too big a risk—he is concerned we have not used Dr Garabaldi before, and Dante is still at large. He suggests you wait until the maternity team you ordered has arrived on Isla Donna.'

My already volatile temper flared. I had no intention of waiting days to have Mia checked over. This was *my* child.

'Fuck Dante. If he comes anywhere near Mia, I will shoot him myself,' I said.

'Gattuso also says that Garabaldi speaks English, and Mia might…'

'She will do what I say,' I snapped, losing the last of my patience at Lorenzo's continued questions. 'Find her a pair of shoes and escort her to the car. I wish to be on Isla Donna before dawn breaks,' I added, knowing I could not get her myself or I would lose what was left of my sanity. I was still aroused, and I needed to get that reaction under control before I dealt with her again. Ironic, given that I had intended to use her desire for me against her, but now I was the one on a damn knife edge.

Lorenzo nodded, but before he could carry out my orders, I added, 'Don't question my authority again, Lorenzo. And do not restrain her. If she refuses to obey you, call me.'

But as he headed to the plane to collect Mia, I knew it wasn't his disobedience that was making me so edgy. It was the woman whose scent had haunted my senses for months now, whose safety was now my responsibility. And who refused to do a damn thing I told her. That would have to end, but the way she had looked at me with challenge but also hurt in her eyes had stirred something in my gut that felt dangerous.

Whatever the hell that emotion was, I would not give in to it.

And Mia would accept her new reality…or she would remain tied to my bed until she did.

CHAPTER TEN

Mia

As the limousine drove through the nighttime streets of Naples—with Vito brooding on the other side of the car, ignoring me as he sent a series of texts, his thumbs flying over his phone—I had the brutal recollection of the last time I'd been with him in the city. The helicopter ride to his estate, the gun battle at dawn, that feeling of exhilaration, of being more alive and terrified than I had ever been before or since.

Weirdly, I wasn't terrified anymore. In fact, I felt strangely calm. I observed the chic, happy people still partying only a few hours before dawn in the sidewalk cafes and nightspots we passed. Their lives seemed so much less complicated than mine. Not that I would have risked hurting my baby, but would they help me if I jumped out of the car? Somehow I doubted it. And what would be the point anyway? Vito would still know I carried his child no matter what I did now.

'Where are we going?' I asked.

Vito looked up from his phone. His eyes narrowed.

Wasn't I even allowed to ask a question?

'I thought we'd be on a boat by now…' I prompted.

He'd mentioned an island, after all. Last night, I had hoped there might be some kind of law enforcement by the docks so I could alert them to my predicament, but was that really an option? As upset as I still was with Vito for kidnapping me, and as determined as I was not to let him take my freedom away, did I really want to see him hurt or imprisoned?

He stared at me, gauging whether he could trust me with the information.

I waited, refusing to relinquish eye contact. He could only bully me if I let him.

Eventually he said grudgingly. 'We will take a helicopter to Isla Donna from the Naples palazzo, but first we must make a stop in the city.'

'What for?' I asked, surprised he had deigned to give me this much.

His gaze zeroed in on my abdomen. 'I have made an appointment with the top obstetrician in the city.'

'In the middle of the night?' I asked, then realised how gauche I sounded when his lips twisted into a cynical smile.

He didn't reply, but then, he didn't have to—when he wanted something, he got it.

But why had he made the appointment? Was he concerned about having manhandled me in London? Somehow I doubted that, given he'd had no qualms about tying me to the bed on the plane, then bringing me to an earth-shattering orgasm.

The car stopped outside a large ornate neoclassical building with a gold plaque on the wall outside announcing it as A Garabaldi's practice. Lorenzo opened the door and Vito got out, then leaned into the car and held out his hand. 'Come, Mia.'

I stared at his outstretched fingers but refused to take them.

'I'm healthy. There's no need for me to see a doctor,' I said, not wanting to engage with the possibility he cared about my health, or the baby's, scared it would weaken my position even more if I began to hope for something that wasn't there. 'I have a midwife at home who's been looking after my antenatal care.'

'You will not be seeing her again, Mia,' he said, his voice tight, but the tone a tiny bit less arsey than usual. 'I have arranged for medical care on the island, but it will take a few days to set up the equipment and hire the staff. Until then, I must ensure you and the baby are well.'

Did he truly care about me, about the baby?

I swallowed, the rawness in my throat—and the sting of emotion—disturbing me. Surely that reaction could only be due to the tumultuous events of the past eight hours. Being kidnapped could make anyone emotional, especially someone whose hormones were totally out of whack.

How could he care about me when he had kidnapped me?

What if my hope that he did care was a layover from that little girl who had wondered occasionally what her dad might be like—and if he might change his mind one day and suddenly appear to claim me as his?

I'd killed those idiotic daydreams a long time ago, and I was much stronger for it. My dad, whoever the hell he was, had been a deadbeat. No surprise there. I wasn't responsible for his choices. I was only responsible for my own. And letting that naive hope in again now, that need for a man's approval, would be the worst possible thing to do when I was already vulnerable enough.

He snapped his fingers, making me jump. '*Vieni*, Mia. We do not have all night.'

The impatient demand cauterised the sting of emotion.

I climbed out—deciding it was best to get the exam over with—but ignored his helping hand to make a point.

I was tired and out of sorts and my emotions far too close to the surface, meaning attempting to figure out Vito's motivations tonight was not a good idea—especially as I was struggling to make sense of my own.

Vito placed a controlling hand on my lower back to usher me into the building and up the stairs, while his men stood guard outside.

The warm, heavy weight of his palm sent a wave of sensation through my already overwrought body, and I shuddered. He sensed the reaction I couldn't disguise. His hand travelled down to cup my bottom, making me even more aware of that proprietary touch.

'Your body knows you are mine, Mia,' he murmured against my neck as we reached the landing. He opened the door without knocking. 'Even if you refuse to accept it.'

Heat spread up my neck, the denial locked in my throat behind the unwanted ball of emotion, as Vito directed me into the doctor's surgery.

An older man appeared, his face flushed. He bowed his head, and they had a conversation in Italian—his tone was obsequious, while Vito's was curt.

The doctor didn't introduce himself to me. He simply nodded profusely and led us both into a large back room where the lights had been dimmed and the shutters closed. Although there was a couch and an examination table, as well as a lot of expensive state-of-the-art equipment including what looked like an ultrasound machine, the room smelled of lavender and fresh linen and was luxuriously decorated. A far cry from the tiny midwife's office in my local clinic back home.

The obstetrician handed me a gown and said in perfect English, 'Please take off your clothing and get on the examination table.' But he didn't make eye contact.

I could sense his fear, though. What had Vito threatened him with to get him to see me at this hour, I wondered? Then tried not to think about it. I already knew how ruthless Vito was. Dwelling on it wasn't going to make my life easier.

As I went to put on the gown, Vito seated himself in an armchair with a view of the examination table, clearly planning to watch the whole thing. I tried not to let it intimidate me. He was the father of this child, and not acknowledging that fact until now had been a mistake.

But as he lounged in the armchair, it made me think of a panther watching his prey. His gaze raked over me with that unsettling combination of awareness and arrogance. The devastating once-over had sensation sinking into my abdomen again as I headed to the screen in the far corner of the room.

I stripped as quickly as I could. The gown was one of those surgical things which was wide open at the back, so I kept my panties on. Even so, I felt hopelessly exposed as the doctor helped me to climb onto the examination table. As I sat there feeling small, aware of Vito watching me, the doctor asked me a series of routine questions while he checked my blood pressure, reflexes, breathing and a whole host of other things the midwife in London had never bothered with. Exhaustion started to overwhelm me, the obstetrician's calm, patient voice soothing in the shadowy room, the questions similar to ones I had answered before about my medical history.

'What was the date of your last menstruation?' he asked softly as he finished taking a series of blood samples and untied the tourniquet.

Before I could remember the answer, though, Vito replied from the shadows in Italian, '*Il bambino è stato concepito il dieci maggio.*'

I'd almost forgotten he was there. But my tired mind translated the relevant words *bambino, concepito* and *dieci maggio* as the doctor scribbled the information in his notes.

Vito leant into the pool of light cast by the lamp beside his chair to rest forearms roped with muscle on his knees. The array of tattoos on the tanned skin made him look even wilder and more dangerous as his hot gaze swept over me, branding my skin.

The tenth of May was the night our baby had been conceived. The confidence with which he announced it felt like a declaration of his ownership. Not just of the baby, but also of me.

Brutal emotion blindsided me—the possessiveness in those crystal-blue eyes both terrifying and strangely intoxicating.

The fierce memories of that night, when he had got me pregnant…and all those hazy memories from my childhood, constantly dreaming about the dad I'd made up in my head, who would appear one day and want me—and Evie, even though he wasn't even her dad—and take care of us the way our mum never had, merged in my consciousness.

I shivered and looked away, trapped in that possessive gaze, aware now I was bound to Vito in a way I could never undo. That I wasn't sure I wanted to undo that connection only disturbed me more.

'Lie down and I will do a scan,' the doctor said, snapping me out of my own thoughts.

But as I lay back, I was far too aware of Vito's watchful presence. My emotional state was so raw my skin felt tight, while my sex was still felt tender from Vito's attentions on the plane.

The doctor switched on the equipment and lubricated the probe. I listened to the mechanical hum of the machine booting up and tried not to read too much into the intimacy of this moment, when Vito would see our baby for the first time.

I stared at the ceiling to gather myself, blinking back the tears that wanted to leak out as the doctor lifted the robe to expose my belly while carrying on a conversation in Italian with Vito.

Vito was asking a lot of questions, none of which I could understand.

The cold wand was placed on my belly. The rapid pulse of the baby's heartbeat filled the room.

I turned my head to stare at the monitor. Brutal emotion overwhelmed me again. Unlike the scans I'd had in London, this machine's picture quality was much clearer and gave a three-dimensional image of my uterus. I could see the baby's face, its features, its tiny hands and fingers, the curve of its spine as it curled in on itself.

Love washed through me—swiftly followed by fear— as I realised how vulnerable that little life was. And how easily it could be harmed. Then a stark, damning realisation followed. How could I ever have believed I could protect this baby on my own?

The doctor spoke in Italian, clearly giving Vito all the information I wanted to hear too. I lifted my head to ask them to speak in English, but what I saw on Vito's face as he watched the pictures on the monitor shocked me into silence. He was staring at the image as he fired questions at the doctor in Italian, but the cynical smile was gone. For the first time since he had appeared in my kitchen, I caught a glimpse of the man I had coaxed out of hiding five long months ago. The man who had taken me with such passion, but had also been playful and even tender as well as dominant.

'What is the doctor saying?' I whispered, desperate not to break that spell.

Vito's gaze lurched to mine. He blinked as if waking from a trance. But the shimmer of wonder remained for a few seconds more. And foolish hope blossomed under my breastbone.

However ruthless he was, however dominating and controlling, seeing his child for the first time *had* had an impact on him.

'He says you and the foetus are healthy and strong. But the baby is large, and you are small.'

My heart lurched at the pride in his voice.

Before he said anything more, though, the doctor began to take a series of measurements with the equipment, interrupting us to relay the information to Vito in Italian.

They continued their conversation, deliberately excluding me. A chill prickled over my skin as they discussed my baby as if I wasn't even there.

The moment of connection felt lost, the tears welling again as I lay back down. And it occurred to me that however strong a connection Vito felt for this baby, he did not necessarily have one to me. The feeling of powerlessness returned full force.

I'd always considered myself so strong—smart and resilient and focussed and adaptable—because I'd had to be as a kid, as a teenager, even as an adult. I'd got over the fact my dad hadn't cared enough about me to stick around and see me born. I'd picked up the pieces when Mum had disappeared when Evie and I were both still teenagers and worked my butt off to make a stable, secure life for us. My ill-advised engagement to Dave had all been part of that plan. Dave might be boring, but he was safe, reliable, predictable. And when I'd discovered he wasn't, I'd kicked him to the curb. During my wild night with Vito, I'd finally discovered sometimes safe could also be repressed. I'd even managed to drag myself up by my bootstraps and get over the trauma of watching Vito get shot, of being shot at myself, once I'd discovered I was pregnant.

But what did I do now? The problems I faced felt insurmountable. What if I really was no more than a piece of 'property' to Vito? How did I deal with the fact I still felt drawn to him—physically, sexually and even emotionally?

I was so screwed. I was rudderless, dependent in a way I'd never been before. And that scared me even more than thinking about all the ways my baby could be hurt in the violent world in which Vito lived. The world I would have to live in now too.

'Leave us.' Vito's command had me drawing in a shattered breath as it dragged me back to the present.

The doctor obeyed him instantly, hooking the wand back to the machine. He switched off the monitor and left the room without another word.

I continued to stare at the screen through the mist which had formed in my eyes. The picture was gone, the monitor dark, but it felt as if I could still hear my baby's heartbeat.

Vito stood and walked towards me. I cradled my bump, aware of the cold gel the doctor hadn't had a chance to wipe off. But when I tried to draw the gown back over my belly, he clasped my wrist, preventing me. Without saying anything, he ripped a strip of tissue off the roll by the machine with his other hand and then slowly cleaned off the gel.

I shuddered, his tender care of me as disconcerting as it was unsettling. I was scared to let my guard down, to let in any feelings towards him. But how could I prevent it when I'd seen the awe on his face before he'd had a chance to mask it? How did I protect myself from that?

He placed his large hand over my stomach. And his gaze rose to my face—the fierce expression devastating me even more.

'It is a boy,' he said, his voice thick with pride.

I nodded as my belly bottomed out under his hand.

'Is that what you wanted?' I asked. A man as alpha as he was would no doubt prize a son more than a daughter. But he seemed surprised by my observation.

'Why would you think this?'

I shrugged. 'Because you're a mafia boss, and from what I've observed of how things operate in your world, men have a lot more power.' Which had to be the understatement of the century.

It saddened me to realise he might not have valued a girl child…even though I might have been better off. Would he have discarded us both if I wasn't carrying his son?

Maybe that's why your own dad didn't want you?

The little voice I remembered from the darkest days of my childhood when my insecurities had got the better of me whispered in my head.

I shut it out because it wasn't going to help me. But then my mind started to race with thoughts of what it could mean for a boy, having Vito as a father. Would he expect his son to inherit his empire? Would he want to teach him how to shoot a gun, how to kill?

I pressed a hand to my mouth and turned away from him, feeling exhausted and overwhelmed. But he grasped my wrist to tug my hand down. Then he gripped my chin to bring my gaze back to his.

'You are wrong, Mia. I am not a monster,' he murmured.

'How do I know that?' I blurted out. 'When I don't know you or what you intend to do with us both?'

He frowned, but instead of looking angry, he ran his thumb down my cheek—his eyes shadowed with an emotion I couldn't name. Not regret, but also not the ruthlessness I was used to. For a second I saw something sad, almost haunted in his eyes.

'Is this why you did not tell me of the baby, because you thought I would hurt you both?'

It would have been so easy in that moment to pretend I had been afraid of him. But I had to be honest with myself now, as well as him, so I shook my head. 'It wasn't you I was afraid of. It was the violence in your life. It terrified me that night, seeing you get shot. I thought if I kept the baby a secret, we would both be safe, that no one would ever find us...'

'This is foolish, Mia. I have enemies. It is a hazard of my business, and they would have found out about you both eventually...'

'But how?' I asked, my voice breaking.

'Stop this,' he said, the dictator returning, but he still didn't sound as angry as he had been before, when he had first spotted my pregnancy. Instead he sounded concerned and determined. 'It is my job to keep you safe. No one can hurt what is mine. I will not let them. You should not have denied me that right…'

What is mine… Why did that sound so cold—and so divorced from the man who had watched his baby on the monitor for the first time only moments ago with awe in his eyes, or the man who had cleaned the gel off so tenderly?

Who was the real Vito Rocco? And how much of myself would I have to risk to find out? Because it felt like I'd risked so much already.

'You talk about the baby and me as if we are possessions you own, Vito,' I said, trying to make him understand how diminished I felt. 'And I hate that. It makes me feel so powerless.'

He stiffened, and those dark brows jerked up his forehead. Was he astonished I had dared to challenge him? Or simply shocked I would expect him to consider the emotional impact of his actions?

I soon realised it might be both when he replied, his tone tight with frustration again.

'You will not be powerless once you accept that you and the baby are my responsibility now. Your feelings will not keep you safe. I will. If you do as I demand, you will have everything a woman could desire.'

'Everything? Really?' I scoffed at the arrogant statement, letting the surge of temper cover the anxiety making my stomach hurt.

He lived a lavish lifestyle, and anything he wanted that he couldn't buy, he took by force—like the services of a top obstetrician in the middle of the night. But I had to make him understand, I wasn't for sale at any price.

'I will be generous with you once you accept your position,' he continued, misunderstanding me again. 'Even though you did not tell me of my child.'

A muscle pulsed in his jaw, signalling his growing anger. The mention of my decision not to tell him about the baby again, though, was a red flag I knew I had to address.

I hadn't been blameless in what had happened up to this point.

I sighed. 'I was wrong not to tell you about the baby,' I conceded. I'd already tried to explain to him why I hadn't told him, but I knew my fear for the baby's safety wasn't the only reason. 'My own father never wanted me. I never even met him,' I managed, hating that admitting it made me feel even more vulnerable. But I wanted him to understand where I was coming from. 'The truth is, I didn't really consider you had rights too where the baby was concerned, and I should have. I guess I just assumed you wouldn't care, that when you said you wanted me gone, that meant you didn't want to see me again, and I apologise for that.'

His brows rose again, but the muscle in his jaw stopped twitching.

'I do care. I care very much that my child is safe,' he said forcefully, and I could see he meant it. 'I am sorry your father chose not to protect you, Mia. My father was not able to protect me also, when I was a boy, because my mother ran from him…' The gruff words hit me hard. Was that why he had been so angry with me? But before the bubble of hope could expand, he continued, his tone as harsh as the resentment in his eyes. 'You must not fight me when I know what is best for you.'

'But can't you see, that makes me a prisoner. I don't

want to give up my freedom, my choices. I won't,' I blurted out, too distressed and heartsore now to be cautious.

The muscle in his jaw tensed again, and his brows lowered.

'Freedom is overrated,' he ground out. His gaze roamed over me, fierce arousal turning the deep blue of his irises to black—and making me brutally aware I was all but naked under the thin robe. 'And it is not what you need.'

I stared back at him, willing the spurt of temper at his arrogant statement to cover the hurt at his refusal to bend. I'd told him about my daddy issues. I'd even apologised for not telling him about the baby, and yet it wasn't enough.

It was obvious we were talking at cross-purposes, that he just didn't get it. But I was suddenly too weary, and frankly too emotional, to press the point. Especially as I could see the heat in his eyes and knew exactly what that meant.

He placed his hand on my thigh under the gown and ran his thumb along the leg of my panties, confirming my suspicions.

'Do you wish me to remind you again what you need— as I did on the plane?' he murmured, the comment as potent as it was provocative.

'No… I don't,' I said, even as sensation pulsed and throbbed in my sex.

Sex and dominance were his go-to ways of controlling me. But what was seriously hot in the bedroom was a lot less hot out of it. And separating the two was the only way I was going to be able to figure out a way through this.

Disappointment flashed in his eyes, but to my surprise, he took his hand off my leg and smoothed down the gown. 'Later,' he said.

I tried to see it as a sign that our relationship had evolved, at least enough to stop him using our chemistry to shore up his position of power, as he helped me to climb off the examination table. But then he hooked my hair behind my ear and cradled my chin. The gesture was so disarming, my heart stuttered.

'Do not be sad, Mia.' His hand trailed down— proprietary, possessive, but also strangely tender, almost reverent when he cradled the bump. 'As the mother of my son, you will always be taken care of.'

I wasn't sure if he realised the qualifier made it clear it was the baby who was important to him, not me. But I couldn't deny the forceful feeling of connection. And the memory of his gaze when he had stared at the images of our child.

Perhaps I should start there. For a hard man, he was genuinely moved at the thought of being a father. And we *did* have a connection outside sex. Neither of us had had a father's protection. That had to mean something, didn't it?

Maybe this wasn't just the desire to mark me as his. Maybe it could be more than that. He had feelings. He had emotions, even if he controlled them so rigidly. Maybe it wasn't completely unreasonable to assume the connection he felt towards this child could be a way behind that shield of dominance and demand he kept around the rest of his emotions.

I nodded, stupidly close to tears again as he pressed a kiss to my forehead, then gave me a light swat on the backside that made me jump. 'Now get dressed. We must leave for Isla Donna.'

To my surprise, he strode out of the room, allowing me to dress in private.

As I walked back to the screen, though, I noticed a phone on the doctor's desk.

I could use it—to ring the police, to ring Evie and explain where I was…

But as soon as the thought occurred to me, I knew I couldn't do it.

Ringing Evie in the middle of the night, when I couldn't explain coherently what was happening would only make her freak out more.

And ringing the police felt wrong.

Maybe it was the memory of Vito's patient touch. Maybe it was the roller coaster of exhausting emotions I'd been on since spotting him in my flat what felt like several lifetimes ago. Maybe it was that I knew however scared I was of Vito's world, he *was* the only person who could keep me and the baby safe now…or maybe it was the small confidences we'd shared, however reluctantly, that gave me hope.

But as I got dressed and walked out of the examination room without making the call which could set me free from him, I knew I had turned a corner. I wasn't going to try and escape again. I had to try and make this work for me and my baby. I would have to guard my heart, but I'd learned how to do that a long time ago. And I'd never been a hopeless romantic like Evie. Practicality and pragmatism had always been my superpowers.

But at the same time, I could not submit to Vito's determination to dominate everyone and everything, especially me. Or he would never respect me, and more importantly, I would never respect myself. Even if I now suspected his determination to dominate me went a lot deeper than just a desire to keep our baby safe.

Somehow, I had to get behind his cast-iron control and discover more of the man I had glimpsed that night and this evening. A man who wasn't a brick wall, incapable of compromise or empathy.

As I entered the outer office, the rush of emotion felt real and valid when he swung round from his hushed conversation with the obstetrician, as if sensing my presence.

He reached out his hand, but then he ruined it by snapping his fingers. '*Vieni*, Mia, we must leave.'

I tensed but resisted the urge to snap back. I'd exhausted all my sass for one night.

So I took his hand without an argument. Surprise crossed his features, and I gave myself a mental high-five. In our battle of wills, surprise was probably my best weapon. Because it might make him start to see me as an autonomous person instead of a woman he now owned.

He escorted me down the stairs and into the waiting limousine—his wide palm resting securely on my back.

I snuggled into my side of the car and yawned. Pulling out his phone, he started to talk to someone in rapid Italian, obviously giving orders again.

I had been dismissed, I realised when we got to his heavily guarded estate—and he hadn't spoken to me once. But I was oddly grateful for the reprieve.

The car drove towards the villa—which looked untouched now after the incident five months ago—and stopped at the heliport on the lawn where we had landed. The huge black chopper was waiting for us, its giant blades already turning. Lorenzo escorted me on board while Vito spoke to a couple of the men with assault rifles standing guard before boarding too.

The echoes of our first night together only made the whole thing seem more surreal as the enormous black bird lifted into the night sky, then hovered over the city and headed out over the bay. My stomach bounced into my throat as we powered across the dark water towards Capri and beyond, and I glanced at the man beside me, his harsh, handsome features set in stark lines by the blinking red light on the helicopter.

Vito Rocco was a force of nature. Taking him on was liable to require all my strength and resilience and a lot of stamina—which meant conserving my energy and choosing my battles more carefully.

Eventually the shape of an island appeared on the horizon, a cluster of lights sprinkled over one end.

'This is Isla Donna,' he said over the headphones, the pride in his voice unmistakable.

As the helicopter travelled along the coastline, a series of secluded coves and rocky headlands were visible in the moonlight, until the big bird touched down next to a palatial villa. Starkly modern in comparison to the neoclassical elegance of Vito's home in Naples, the stunning white stone-and-glass structure was larger and even more opulent, perched on the edge of a promontory with steps leading down the cliff face. An array of marble terraces looked out onto a sea view which would be spectacular in the daylight. On the lowest terrace was a large floodlit infinity pool, its water a glowing turquoise in the darkness.

He pressed his palm to the small of my back again to lead me down the helicopter steps, and we were greeted by a group of household staff. But when he propelled me through a high stone archway into a marble foyer, I pulled away from that proprietary touch.

'I'd like to sleep alone tonight,' I said.

He frowned, obviously having intended to lead me straight to his bed. I bristled at his arrogance.

That he had assumed he had me exactly where he wanted me—and I was going to do everything he demanded from now on—didn't surprise me. But that he hadn't intended to ask what I wanted only made me more aware of the mountain I still had to climb.

'There is no way off this island, Mia, if you think to run from me again,' he said, but his tense expression gave me a glimmer of hope. That he didn't trust me was obvious, but all I wanted right now was some space—and a chance to get a good night's sleep. If he could respect that much, it was a start.

Baby steps, Mia.

'I'm not planning on going anywhere tonight,' I offered. 'I'm shattered,' I added just as my mouth broke into a huge yawn.

He didn't look happy, but a wave of relief gushed through me when he beckoned a girl from the row of staff waiting to serve him in the foyer—and spoke to her in Italian.

The maid bowed and blushed, calling him *padrino* several times—and making me brutally aware that every single person on this island was at his beck and call... No wonder he expected me to be at his beck and call, too. That he hadn't refused my request, though, felt huge.

'Gabriella will show you to one of the guest suites... for tonight,' he announced.

'Thank you,' I murmured, grateful for the respite, at least until the morning.

When she went to lead me away, though, he grasped my wrist and tugged me back to face him. '*A domani,*

Mia,' he said, sweeping his thumb over my rampaging pulse.

Until tomorrow.

I didn't speak much Italian, but I understood that much.

I could see the challenge in his eyes, hear the warning in his voice, and feel the inevitable surge of awareness, despite my tiredness… His eyes darkened when I nodded and tugged my hand free, and I knew he'd felt it too.

I followed Gabriella to a stunning, lavishly furnished suite with its own terrace. The hazy light of dawn glowed red on the horizon. But as I collapsed onto the bed and sank into oblivion, I was well aware that even if I had won this small battle, I had in no way won the war. Because my sex was already aching with emptiness again—and my emotions were still in uproar.

CHAPTER ELEVEN

Vito

'Don Vito, I am sorry to disturb you, but we have a problem…'

I glanced up from the report I was reading over lunch on the syndicate's money-laundering operations in Europe, to find the head of my household staff standing on my private terrazzo. Allegra's flustered expression did not bode well, nor did the panicked look of the girl behind her who had been assigned to care for Mia late last night.

I paid Allegra well because she did not get flustered. *What the fuck has Mia done now?*

I slapped the laptop closed and stood up, the familiar punch of temper and awareness flowing through me.

'What problem, Allegra?' I demanded, but I could already guess.

I should have known Mia's subdued behaviour last night after the scan had been a ruse. Why had I trusted her?

'When Gabriella went to check on the signorina five minutes ago, she was not to be found.'

Annoyance came first, swiftly followed by the hollow feeling in my chest that I despised—and which I had noticed again last night, when Mia had told me of her *bastardo* of a father with a beseeching look in her eyes.

'I am so sorry, *padrino*. I searched everywhere, but there is no sign…' The girl behind Allegra began to babble, terrified at having displeased me.

'*Va bene.*' I held up my hand to cut her off before she became hysterical.

My staff knew I expected their loyalty, always, and that if I gave an order, it must be obeyed. But it was not this girl's fault Mia had chosen to defy me. Or that she had somehow managed to lull me into believing she would do as she was told from now on.

She had been exhausted and emotional in the doctor's office. In truth, I had been struggling with a reaction I had not expected myself at the sight of the child growing inside her. *My son.* The fierce feeling of connection, of protectiveness towards that tiny, defenceless life, and the woman who nurtured it had shocked me. Enough that I had let my control slip and been softer than I should have been with her.

I should not have let her have her own suite last night. But the desire to hold her, to possess her again, to mark her as mine, had been so visceral, I had chosen not to indulge it. I could see she was tired.

The doctor had assured me penetrative sex was perfectly okay—it was one of the reasons I had wanted to have Mia checked before we arrived on the island. I was a big man, and I had been concerned my need for her might hurt the baby. But I had not expected to see the child so clearly in those images.

As we had flown to Isla Donna, though, I had decided it was normal to feel a connection to my own flesh and blood—as I had told her, I was not a monster. But when she had told me of her father, I had let sentiment weaken my resolve. I would not let it happen again.

Yes, my world was dangerous. That was simply a fact of life. And as I had tried to make her understand, to survive in this life—the rewards of which were great—I was prepared to be ruthless.

All that talk about her choices, her freedom, had no place here, and the sooner she accepted that, the better. In this life there was only money, strength, sex and death. Everything else was a luxury I did not care to indulge.

I had loved my mother as a boy, and it had not improved her lot or mine one iota. I had also loved Dante as a brother, but it had not prevented him from attacking me. Nor would it save him when my men captured him.

Mia had chosen to have my child, but it was past time she understood that was where her choices ended.

Her bravery and boldness in challenging my control had earned my grudging respect. I could not deny it. But I did not intend to let her defy me again.

'Should I contact Lorenzo and have the island searched?' the housekeeper asked.

I shook my head. The last damn thing I needed was to have Mia disturb everyone's peace. The men were tired. They had been working long shifts for months now, not to mention the injuries some of them had sustained during Dante's attack. And the hunt for that bastard remained ongoing. I suspected he had gone to ground in his estate near Sicily. The Malvini family, his mother's family, had been little more than a street gang when he had fought his way to the top of their ranks as a boy of fifteen, seven years after he and his mother had been expelled from the Rocco Syndicate by my father.

It was a sorry affair, and I couldn't help thinking now,

after seeing my own son on that monitor, I would not have been able to discard my child so easily. But then, my father's ruthlessness had made us all rich.

It would be a waste of manpower to storm Dante's stronghold, but he would have to leave eventually. When he did, I would be waiting. Until that day, though, my men deserved a rest—which meant not spending a day searching the island for a pregnant girl who could not have gone far.

I stared out at the searing blue water, my chaotic heartbeat slowing.

Isla Donna was my sanctuary, the place my father had brought me after rescuing me from my stepfather. The place where I had grown the Rocco Syndicate into an empire of legal and illegal enterprises which spanned all of Europe and was making in-roads now in North and South America. The place where I had come to lick my wounds after the attack, the place where my child would be born and Mia would remain until I tired of her. When that happened, she would be provided for, as long as she obeyed the strictures placed on her for her safety and that of our child.

But as my gaze scanned the coastline, my irritation turned to something that felt akin to panic at the thought Mia might be contrary enough to attempt to swim the five-mile distance to Capri.

Could she really be so desperate to escape me?

Then something caught my eye in the small cove directly below the terrazzo.

Mia. Che cazzo?

What the actual...?

I swore under my breath. Then anxiety gripped my

chest, which only made me angrier with her. And with myself.

I had given her space, out of respect for her condition and to give her time to adjust to her situation after last night's emotional overload, which was another sign of weakness. But I would not trust her again.

'The signorina will be staying in my rooms from now on,' I growled as I marched across the wide terrazzo. My housekeeper and the maid rushed off to make the necessary arrangements—at least someone around here knew the consequences of defying me. While I headed down the steps in the cliff wall which led to the private beach, my fury increased with each step.

She would regret making me angry. She had brought this on herself by trying to trick me. She would soon learn, trust had to be earned. And until she earned mine—which was going to take several millennia the way she was going—the safest place for her was in my bed as I rocked us both to orgasm.

She had made it clear by her actions it was the only place in my world where she belonged, and where I could guarantee to keep her out of trouble.

Mia

I stared as a powerboat motored past the end of the cove. Two men stood on the deck, assault rifles thrown casually over their shoulders, while another armed man scanned the horizon with a set of binoculars.

My heartbeat pounded into my throat.

Isla Donna wasn't an island. It was a fortress. I looked

down at my bare feet sinking into the wet sand, my pulse ramping up as the boat disappeared past the rocky headland covered in the dark pink blossoms of bougainvillea.

The island's spellbinding beauty, the profusion of wildflowers and this deserted beach nestled in a rocky cove beneath the lavish villa above, seemed so peaceful, so calm and relaxing. But for the vivid reminder of who owned this island.

I lifted the light linen negligée I'd found in the suite's armoire. It looked brand-new—had it belonged to someone else before me? How many other women had Vito brought to his island? The sting of jealousy was lowering. How much of a claim did I really have on him, despite the pregnancy? How much did I even want? We'd been thrown together by fate—and while I now knew he felt a deep sense of responsibility towards his child, there was no evidence yet he would ever feel that for me.

I huffed out a careful breath.

God, I had so many questions I was too scared to ask myself, let alone him.

But there was no getting away from the fact anymore. My life had fundamentally changed now. Deciding to have Vito's baby hadn't really been a choice. The minute I'd realised our reckless night together had had unforeseen consequences, I'd felt the surge of love for my child. For *his* child. But had there been more to that visceral longing to keep my unborn baby? Would I have felt the same way about an accidental pregnancy with Dave, even though we had planned to marry? I really didn't think so. And the implications of that bothered me even more than having to figure out how I was going to find a place in Vito's world.

The shallow waves caused by the boat's wake lapped

to shore and splashed over my shins, wetting the hem of the negligée. I dug my toes into the sand, absorbing the rough texture and the cool water on my hot skin, and stepped farther into the surf.

I'd woken from a deep sleep twenty minutes ago, surprisingly refreshed, even as the throbbing ache in my sex reminded me of everything that had happened the day and night before…and with whom.

Vito's face—dark, dangerous and devastating—had haunted my dreams. Another sign the chemistry we shared had always had a powerful effect on my psyche. As well as my libido.

I gathered my hair up to enjoy the sea breeze on my sweaty neck and took another step into the ocean, keen to cool more of my heated skin.

Even if it hadn't been for the armed guards patrolling the sea around the island, I'd already decided last night I wasn't going anywhere. I laid my hand on my bump, aware of the flicker of movement I'd felt again that morning when I'd woken up.

My baby, *our* baby, would be safer here than anywhere else. But that didn't mean I was going to give up any more of my autonomy.

My main order of business today was to get Vito to let me contact Evie. She would be worried sick about where I was. My sudden disappearance would no doubt bring back memories for her of the morning our mum had just buggered off and left us. Would she guess who I was with? That I hadn't had a choice? Or would she think I'd abandoned her too, without even leaving a note? The thought made guilt and regret twist in my gut. And my anger with Vito's high-handed behaviour returned.

Another wave slapped against my thighs, making me gasp, just as a shout rang out behind me.

'Mia, *fermati.*'

I swung round to see Vito running across the sand, his saturnine features set in the same grim lines of fury I remembered from when he'd first spotted my pregnancy.

Before I had a chance to process what had made him so angry this time, he had splashed into the sea. Covering us both in sea water, he scooped me into his arms, forcing me to grab hold of his neck as he marched back towards the shore.

'Vito, what are you doing?' I said, my pulse charging into my throat.

'You little fool, I will tie you to the bed again if I have to,' he growled, his breathing ragged as he deposited me on the sand, then grasped my arms to drag me towards him until my belly was pressed against his flat abs.

He was soaked, and so was I, the water making our light clothing transparent. I was suddenly brutally aware I had nothing but a pair of panties on under the negligée. I hadn't bothered to get dressed properly. When I'd spotted the deserted, secluded beach below the suite's terrace, I'd just wanted some time alone, a chance to get my wayward emotions in order and start figuring out how the hell I was going to contact my sister…and convince Vito he couldn't make me a prisoner here.

But all the arguments to persuade Vito to let me call Evie and get him to respect my autonomy, which I had been working on since waking up, got trapped in my throat now, because we were virtually naked on an empty beach in bright sunlight, and I was too aware of the way my nipples were throbbing incessantly. I could see the outline of his cock through the soaked linen of his trousers.

Stop looking at that and start figuring out what has got him so furious.

'Don't you ever do that again,' he shouted. I could see not just anger in his eyes now but fear.

'Do what?' I asked, deciding to ignore the threat to tie me up again because he didn't seem rational. And he was tough enough to reason with when he was.

'Swim away from me…' he yelled at me, making no sense at all. 'It is five miles to Capri in tidal waters. There is no way you can get off this island, but I will lock you in my bedroom if you will not keep yourself safe. If that is what you want, that is what you will get.'

I struggled out of his grasp, rubbed my arms where his fingers had gripped, and glared at him—hating that tone of voice, the way he spoke to me as if I was a disobedient child who he got to boss around for my own good.

'What the hell are you talking about, Vito?' I shouted, my voice breaking on the words as all the injustices he had heaped upon me in the last eighteen hours came flooding back—despite all my best intentions to placate him. *Sod that*, he was just bullying me now because he was bigger and stronger than I was, and I wasn't having it.

'I should not have trusted you. I will not trust you again. From now on, you will remain where I can see you at all times.' He grasped my arm again and began marching me back towards the steps cut into the rock face which led back to the villa.

I dug my heels into the sand, to no avail.

'Are you nuts? I wasn't trying to swim to Capri,' I cried, but he just carried on walking, all but dragging me now.

'And why should I believe this?' he demanded. 'When

you have done nothing but defy me at every turn. And put yourself in unnecessary danger.'

'Oh, sod off!' I yelled back, managing to yank my arm from his grasp. 'I don't give a damn if you believe me or not.' I could feel the hysteria rise up my chest.

The caustic, visceral fury was spurred on by a sense of injustice which I had been forced to keep under rigid control my whole life—so I didn't piss off my useless mum, so I didn't scare Evie, so I didn't make a mistake and alert the landlord or the people at the social security office to the fact it was me signing my mum's cheques. So I didn't get into any trouble at school that might make the teachers call my mum, and realise she wasn't there, and hadn't been for months. But I was through being careful, being cautious, being amenable, because with Vito it meant he would simply flatten me like a steamroller and pound what little freedom and autonomy I had left into dust.

'I'm five months pregnant, in case you haven't noticed,' I shouted at him and the look of disapproval on his face. I cradled my bump. 'I would never put *my* baby at risk like that. It's bad enough he has a dangerous, dictatorial arsehole for a father. He doesn't need a reckless idiot for a mother to boot. I happen to know what that's like, and it's not pretty.'

He tensed, but to my surprise, the rigid muscle in his jaw softened, and his glare downgraded a notch. He crossed his arms, making the soaked shirt stretch across his pecs. The swirling ink on his chest was visible beneath the damp cloth—but so was the livid scar slashing across his shoulder. The same shoulder he'd been shot in all those months ago. I stared at the line of stiches, the sympathy welling in my throat again, the way it had that night. How could that have been just a scratch?

'You were not trying to swim to Capri?' he asked, drawing my gaze from his ruined shoulder. The scepticism was still written all over his face, but his tone lacked that dictatorial edge I had come to resent so much.

'Are you actually serious?' I managed, my tone frigid with fury. Because—what the hell? How much of an idiot did he think I was? 'I'm not a good enough swimmer to get as far as the boats full of men with machine guns you've got patrolling the island. Which—FYI—is an even bigger disincentive than the prospect of swimming across five miles of open water while I'm pregnant.' I sucked in a deep breath, let it out, trying to control my breathing, when his gaze drifted down to my breasts, which now felt swollen and tender against the negligée. And far too exposed. My nipples pinched into tight peaks. I glanced down, and heat climbed up my neck. The areolas—already enlarged from my pregnancy—were a dark red, my rigid nipples practically poking through the transparent cloth. That he had noticed too was obvious when his gaze met mine. His pupils had dilated to black, his arousal as fierce as his temper had been moments before.

I folded my arms over my boobs and tried to squeeze them into submission, aware of that hot gaze branding my skin.

'Plus, I realised last night trying to escape from you is probably counterproductive now anyway,' I rasped, my mouth dry.

One dark eyebrow arched, but the fierce approval only made the heat blaze across my collarbones and sink into my needy sex.

'So you have seen sense,' he said in that arsey way he had that made me want to punch him.

I balled my fingers into a fist. Why, even when I was

offering him an olive branch, did he have to be such a controlling jerk?

'There's nothing sensible about this situation,' I said, my temper turbo-charging the heat, not to mention the infuriating thought he was never going to give me an inch…especially if I made the mistake of backing down.

Agreeing not to attempt another escape was one thing, letting him treat me like a prisoner quite another.

'I know my options are limited,' I pointed out, determined to make him see I was making a choice here, not just surrendering to his agenda. 'And as I was with you that night five months ago, when I got a taste of the threats against you…' My gaze dragged over the scar on his shoulder again, and I couldn't help the shiver of horror. 'I've decided the safest option for my baby and me right now is to remain here with you.'

His eyes narrowed, and it was clear he wasn't convinced by my sudden capitulation.

'If you think to trick me, Mia, into trusting you again, so that you can escape, it will not work.'

For fuck's sake…

I ground my teeth, his cynicism and arrogance starting to get on my last nerve.

'Right now, I don't give a crap whether you trust me or not,' I said, wishing I could believe that. Because it was already clear gaining his trust was going to be a very tall order—when he had no doubt spent his life never trusting anyone. 'But if you tie me up again, I will make you pay, when you least expect it… You have been warned.'

His eyebrows shot up his forehead—but then he let out an incredulous laugh. And I wanted to scream, mostly because the threat I'd just issued sounded preposterous even to me.

What exactly was I planning to do, browbeat him to death? The only person I'd ever hit was him, and that was only because he'd tied me up and kidnapped me…and it hadn't even slowed him down, let alone stopped him.

But as I went to march past him, planning to return to my bedroom and sulk for the rest of eternity, he snagged my wrist, tugging me to a stop.

'Don't touch me…' I yanked my hand back to try and shake him off. He simply tightened his grip, holding me still with ease, his strength so much greater than mine. He pulled me round until he could place his hand on my hip. And hold me.

I blinked furiously, close to tears, that devastating feeling of powerlessness mixing with all the pregnancy hormones to push me right to the edge. *Again.*

But instead of issuing another of his bloody ultimatums, he pressed his forehead to mine and let out a deep sigh.

'Shhh, Mia, this is not good for the baby,' he said—with a tenderness I wasn't prepared for.

I drew back to stare into his eyes—the confusion I saw in them shocking me into silence.

I nodded. 'I know.'

I wiped my eyes with my free fist, determined not to let the tears fall. And looked down at my toes again. Maybe this was Stockholm syndrome. Because it seemed when he showed me the slightest bit of care or attention, I became a complete emotional wreck, all my insecurities making me doubt myself…

He tucked a knuckle under my chin, lifting my gaze to his. He brushed a thumb across my bottom lip, making me tremble.

'If you give me your word you will not attempt to run

from me again, I will not tie you to the bed…' he said, but the words were measured, as if he was making a major concession.

A part of me wanted to take the offer so we could get past this. But I knew I couldn't capitulate. He was a man accustomed to using threats and intimidation to get what he wanted. But if I agreed to let him bully me, where would it end? I refused to be his captive. If I was going to be here by choice, I had to stand up to him, always.

I shook my head. 'I told you I wasn't going to run. I told you why. That you don't trust me is your problem, not mine. I'm not going to promise to obey you when you threaten me. Because that's not giving me a choice.'

He frowned, his expression hardening with distrust.

Well, he certainly hadn't expected that. But I didn't care. I couldn't live with his constant disapproval and demands any more than I could live knowing he didn't trust me to keep myself and our baby safe.

I tried to tug my hand free again, but he held firm. The puzzled expression made me wonder how long it had been since anyone refused to play by his rules.

'You are making this more difficult than it needs to be, Mia,' he said.

My pulse went haywire as his callused thumb caressed the inside of my wrist in slow, focussed strokes, that piercing blue gaze intensifying. 'I am not a man who trusts easily…' His gaze dropped to my belly. 'Especially when there is much at stake.'

I shuddered, and his gaze darkened. The melting sensation at my core was familiar, and predictable.

'Perhaps we should simplify this?' he said, his intent clear.

He planned to seduce me again, to make me beg, so

that he could regain the upper hand, so that he could ensure my compliance. Because he knew I didn't have any defence against the sensations he stirred so effortlessly.

But when his free hand rose to cup my breast and he drew his thumb across the hard, aching tip, his touch entitled, possessive, I didn't fight the sensations shooting down to my core or the need flooding my already damp panties. Because I wasn't afraid of this connection anymore.

My back arched, my body instinctively leaning into the caress.

He let out a gruff chuckle, his voice raw with the same hunger already consuming me. He tugged me closer to stroke my neck with his tongue, where my pulse pounded. His arm banded around my back, drawing me flush against him. I writhed against the thick outline of his erection.

'The doctor said it will not harm the baby to fuck you…' He growled against my ear, the crude words startling me.

Was that why he hadn't taken me on the plane, when I had been soaked in afterglow and desperate to feel him inside me again? Not because he had been trying to control me, but because he had been trying to control himself.

The thought sent power lancing through me. The only way he could use this incendiary chemistry against me was if I let him. If I enjoyed it, if I indulged it, if I owned it the way he did, he couldn't use it to control me again.

He kneaded my buttocks, then dragged my leg up to hook it over his hip, dipping slightly to rub the thick erection against the spot where I ached the most through our wet clothing.

'I will not need to tie you down if I keep you riding my

cock, Mia,' he groaned, the words meant to intimidate me—but the strain I could see on his face only made me feel bolder. This desperate hunger, this elemental need made us equal because the desire to quench it was unstoppable now for both of us.

I clasped his cheeks, brought his gaze to mine, dry humping him for all I was worth, to relieve the empty ache in my sex—and not ashamed to let him know it.

'Do I have your word on that, Vito?' I demanded, throwing his own ultimatum back at him.

Astonishment flashed across his features, swiftly followed by hunger…and admiration.

My heartbeat thundered against my ribs.

Although I lacked his physical strength, and could never be as ruthless or as dangerous, I had bested Vito at his own game—simply by matching his demands with demands of my own. Demands I knew now I would never be ashamed of again.

'You little witch,' he barked, lifting me effortlessly into his arms, clasping my hips and forcing me to wrap my legs around his waist, making me brutally aware of that thick ridge working me into a frenzy. 'I will make you pay for that…'

I sank my fingers into his short hair, dragged his mouth to mine, the desire firing through my nerve endings from everywhere our bodies touched, making me feel powerful and free at last.

'Promises, promises…' I groaned against his lips before covering his hard mouth with mine.

He let out a pained laugh before grasping my head to angle my mouth and take the kiss deep, while holding me aloft with the forearm banded under my bum. He marched towards the rock staircase as we devoured each other, my breasts pressed against his chest, the sweet spot between my thighs weeping in agonised ecstasy at the thought of what was to come.

He stopped abruptly, though, as we reached the cliff steps.

'*Dio*, I cannot carry you up all those stairs before I get inside you. It will kill me, *bella*...' he moaned.

I gazed at him, his desperation making the power charge through me again, burning away the last of my inhibitions. 'Then don't.'

He dropped me to my feet on the sand in a secluded area next to the cliffs, then grasped the neck of my negligée and ripped it down the middle, leaving me trembling and aching and exposed to him. The warmth of the sun on my damp skin was nothing to the fire building inside me. He draped the torn material on the sand and clasped my hand, directing me to lie on the makeshift bed. I did as I was told, his expression so intense it brushed over my skin like a physical caress.

He murmured something in Italian, but I could see the fierce approval in his eyes as he followed me down, his hands stroking my curves, learning me all over again. He hooked his thumbs in my panties, worked them off, then threw them away. Kneeling between my spread thighs, he clasped my bum and lifted my sex to his mouth, licking and kissing the heart of me. I rose to meet his tongue, my clit so swollen already it felt like a boulder between my legs. Unlike before on the plane, when he had been the one in control, coaxing me, destroying me, making me beg, this time he simply devoured me, forcing me to a fast, hard and unforgiving climax in seconds.

The glittering shards pulsed through me, exploding from my core, my mind fraying, my body no longer my own, the power ebbing and flowing as I rode the whirl-wind only he had ever caused.

But when he rose over me, releasing the thick erection from his pants, I pushed up on my elbows to clasp him in my hand.

He groaned again as I ran my fingers from the root to the tip, the pulsing heat of him powerful and overwhelming, but also mine. I slid my thumb across the broad head, gathering the slippery drops of pre-cum, the scent of him addictive. The sight of his face taut with longing and that huge cock jumping from my touch was so erotic it made my sex hurt.

I needed him inside me, now.

He grasped my wrist to stop me from caressing him. '*Troppo*,' he growled. 'It is too much.'

Cradling my hips in hard hands, he forced my knees wide to accommodate him, then palmed the massive erection and pressed it to my slick folds.

'Lie back,' he demanded.

I collapsed onto the sand as he entered me, spreading me wide with the thick girth. The penetration was deep, the stretched feeling too much, but he didn't stop, relentlessly working himself inside me until my muscles relaxed enough to let him in all the way.

I lay shattered, conquered, my breathing coming out in ragged pants, his conquest of me complete.

'Ah, *Dio*,' he groaned, and I knew he was as overwhelmed as me.

Dazed desire darted through my nerve endings, the too-full feeling giving way to exquisite licks of pleasure as he began to move.

He braced himself above me so as not to press against my abdomen. The penetration was too much and yet not enough as each thrust took him deeper. Sensation shimmered, pulsed, that spot deep inside me clenching and releasing in a desperate battle to reach that towering pinnacle.

I clasped his head. 'Vito, more, harder, faster.'

He pressed his hand to my cheek, his gaze fierce. But then he nodded. Grasping my hips, he rolled until suddenly I was on top of him, my knees on either side of his hips, that huge erection seated deep.

'Ride me, Mia,' he demanded, adjusting me, forcing me to sit upright, to take him to the hilt.

The penetration was immense, his cock so deep it felt as if I would choke on it. But as he moved me on him, lifting me up, drawing me down, I began to participate in my own annihilation, chasing the beautiful oblivion galloping towards me.

I rode him as he grasped my breasts, squeezing the sensitive nipples, forcing me into a maelstrom. Sweat glistened, the sounds of our flesh slapping together, the brutal beauty magnificent as I felt him grow even larger inside me.

He roared, lifting into me, hot seed coating my insides as my own brutal climax crested and dragged me into the vortex. I cried out, shattering, riding him for all I was worth before I collapsed on top of him, a sweating, shivering mess.

He clasped my head, holding me against his chest as we sank into the bright cloud together, his heartbeat against my ear thundering as fast and furiously as my own.

My body would always belong to him, I realised, still dazed with afterglow…

But I wasn't afraid of my addiction anymore, because I knew his belonged to me now, too.

CHAPTER TWELVE

Vito

FUCK.

How could the sex be even more intense than it was before? How could I have lost myself completely as soon as she contracted around my cock? Before I had ensured her surrender—which was what I had intended to do when I had spotted her hard nipples beneath the damp cloth, begging for my mouth…

Mia stirred, her sex clasping me—too tight, too exquisite. But as she shifted and attempted to lift off me, I dragged my hands down to cradle her butt and hold her still, before my needy cock surged to life once more

'Do not move yet,' I groaned, aware I was the one having to beg.

She sank back onto my chest and stilled, her staggered breathing audible over the murmur of the tide. But then the rumble of the patrol boat coming around the point forced me to act. The men had binoculars, and although they would not dare to stare at my woman without my permission, I did not want her naked where they might be able to see her.

Rolling over, I covered her body with mine, shielding

her from prying eyes. I threaded her wet hair back from her face, dragged my thumb across her flushed cheek.

My cock twitched again, but I forced myself to pull out of her, then gathered the remnants of her dress to cover her nakedness as best I could. She took the torn cloth in unsteady hands, her fingers trembling.

The satisfaction—that she had been as deeply affected as I had by that insane joining—was short-lived, though. There was not enough cloth to cover the mound of her pregnancy. I stared down at her belly, which only triggered my arousal again.

Standing, I pulled up my trousers and tugged off my wet shirt, then offered her my hand. She took it in silence, allowing me to help her onto her feet, and did not object when I draped my shirt over her shoulders, fed her arms into the sleeves and buttoned it with clumsy fingers.

There, at least she was no longer naked for anyone to see.

'Come,' I said, clasping her hand. 'We must return to the villa,' I continued. 'You will sleep in my bedroom from now on,' I added in a desperate bid to prove I still controlled this situation. Even though I knew I did not.

But if I could get her to my bedroom and keep her there until I got my rampaging heartbeat—and my rampant cock—under control, I would be able to reestablish the power in this relationship. And figure out what had just happened.

Could I believe her? That she had no desire to escape from me now?

Why should I even *want* to risk trusting her, when it would be so much easier not to? If I did not trust her, I could justify keeping her close without having to examine the reasons why.

But instead of doing as I asked, she tugged her hand from my grasp.

'No, Vito,' she said, the mutinous expression familiar. 'I'm not going to let you treat me like a prisoner here. I thought I made that clear.'

I pressed my hand to her stomach, the spurt of panic returning which had propelled me down those steps in the first place.

'If you are telling me the truth—and you are aware you must remain here—then you also know you are mine to protect…' I said. 'And I did not hear you complaining a moment ago when you were full of my cock.'

She stepped back, but what I saw in her eyes—not just temper and embarrassment, but disappointment—had the hollow ache pulsing in my chest again. *Damn her.*

'Stop trying to use sex as a weapon, Vito.' She glanced at my thrusting cock. 'We both wanted it. We both came.'

I swore as desire surged through me again. Aware that somehow she had got the upper hand. Because she was right. I wanted her just as much, and my hunger for her was impossible to hide.

'I'll move into your rooms, but you have to let me call Evie,' she said. 'And I refuse to be a prisoner here. You kidnapped me without clothes, so I would like to return to Naples and buy some more.' Her voice sounded firm, but I could see the wariness in her eyes—as well as the determination. And somehow, it gave me pause.

'Now who is trying to use sex as a weapon, *bella*,' I replied.

No way was she going anywhere near Naples. It was too dangerous, with Dante's exact whereabouts unknown. But my desire to control her didn't seem to matter as much anymore as the desire to take the disappointment out of her eyes.

Which made no damn sense whatsoever. Since when had I ever cared what a woman thought of me? Not since I was a boy, and my mother had begged me to protect her.

And I had failed.

I brushed the brutal recollection to one side, because it had no place in this negotiation.

The blush charged up her neck to incinerate her cheeks, giving me some satisfaction. She was no more in control of the desire which had just crucified us both than I was…

'It's… It's not the same thing. I didn't kidnap you,' she murmured.

There it was again, the defeated tone which made the hollow ache return. The hollow ache I couldn't destroy.

I cupped her cheek, pulled her gaze to mine and gave in to the desire to give her something. 'I will let you contact your sister, but I must witness the exchange.'

I could not trust her, not that much. Some things were non-negotiable.

'And you will not leave the island,' I added.

She clasped my hand to pull it down from her face, but the tremble of emotion in her face seemed to eat into my soul. 'I can't be a prisoner here, Vito. I won't.'

My temper spiked at her reaction. What more did she expect of me?

'I will not compromise your safety, or my own. Naples is too dangerous right now,' I said, not even sure why I was bargaining with her.

Why should I care if she was disappointed in me? What mattered was that I prevented her from doing something foolish. But the plea in her eyes made the hollow ache unbearable when she replied.

'Then let me go somewhere else so I know I'm not a prisoner here.'

I swore in Italian, frustrated beyond belief. 'Fine, you may go to Milan…' Because I owned several properties there and had influence, while Dante had none. 'But *I* will accompany you…'

This too was non-negotiable.

Instead of arguing further, though, tears shimmered in her eyes. Tears of gratitude, I realised when she murmured, 'Thank you, Vito.'

Confusion assailed me, and emotions I had never experienced before. Emotions I did not like.

I had lost control of the situation with these concessions. But I would get it back.

Gripping the lapels of my shirt, I tugged her towards me. I covered her mouth, determined to get control back the only way I knew how.

Her lips opened, and my tongue claimed her. I drove deep, exploiting the soft sobs of her instant surrender. There was only one language we both understood, only one way to make this work. But as she sank into the kiss, giving of herself, her fingers clutching at my shoulders, the scent of her arousal filling my senses… I lost sight of my objective.

Not a problem, I told myself as I swung her into my arms and began the long climb up the stairs to the villa. Each step of the way, I focussed on my physical needs, and my determination to possess her again. I had not lied to her when I had told her that keeping her riding my cock would be the best way to keep her out of trouble…

She could have her damn precious freedom, up to a point. She had fought valiantly for it, and I respected that. And if conceding this much meant she would not run from me again, that she would give herself to me without holding anything back—these small concessions would be worth it.

Mia

'Evie, it's me,' I said when the video call connected.

Evie's face lit up, and the guilt blindsided me. My sister looked exhausted, her usually bright eyes dull from lack of sleep.

'Mia, thank god. I've been so worried. Where the hell...' Evie trailed off as her gaze shifted to the man over my shoulder.

As per our agreement, Vito was sitting behind me, his hands on my abdomen. His thighs bracketing my hips.

He'd insisted on showering with me when we'd reached his suite, and he'd taken me against the wall of the cubicle. The man was insatiable, but then, so was I.

'You contacted him?' Evie asked, confused and wary.

I shifted in his lap.

'Your sister is with me so that I can protect her and our child,' Vito said, his low voice husky with purpose.

'Why didn't you tell me, Mia? Didn't you trust me?' Evie asked, her expression devastated that I hadn't confided in her something which had never happened.

I wanted to kick Vito in that moment for making Evie think even for a second I didn't trust her. But I had to concede it was better for Evie not to know how I had really got to Isla Donna, or she would move heaven and earth to rescue me.

And after everything that had happened, I knew I didn't need to be rescued anymore.

Even though I already suspected my decision to remain with Vito wasn't just about the need to protect my baby. It was also about all those glimpses he had given me of another man. Not just the ruthless, dominating mafia boss, but the man who had risked his life to save mine. And the man who had looked overawed by the sight of his baby in the surgery in Naples last night. The man who had draped his wet shirt over me and carried me up about five hundred stairs as if I were precious. The guy who could make me feel cherished and more alive than I had ever felt before. The man who could bend if I pushed him hard enough.

'I'm sorry, Evie. I didn't know he planned to come and get me,' I said, trying to lie to her as little as possible. 'Until he turned up at the flat yesterday.'

Had it really only been yesterday?

'Are you sure you're okay? Where even are you?' Evie asked, not buying my white lies. 'It's not like you to just disappear. You didn't even take your phone or your shoes with you. It reminded me of when Mum took off…' she continued. Her voice broke, and I could see the panic in her eyes from the day our mother had disappeared.

'I'm in Italy. It was all quite sudden. Vito didn't want to hang around. I'm so, so sorry…' I tried to make amends, to convince her, but before either of us could say more, Vito rode his hand up my bump, tugging me firmly into his lap.

'You must not concern yourself with your sister's welfare,' he said, as if that was even a thing Evie could do, just cut off her feelings for me. 'She is my responsibility now.'

I glanced at him over my shoulder, the weightless feeling in my belly at the possessive tone not helping. 'Vito, please. I need to talk to my sister without you interfering.'

His dark brows flattened. But he didn't object the way I knew he wanted to.

'*Prego*!' he growled, clearly not happy, but willing to give me an inch—which felt like a mile. 'Talk. I will listen.'

The weightless feeling in my belly returned because he had backed down when I'd asked him to and made room for my feelings, even though I knew he wanted to dominate this conversation.

I turned back to Evie, trying not to make too much of it. 'Honestly, I'm good, sis. Vito's arranged maternity care on the island. He's taking care of me…' Heat blasted up my neck as I recalled exactly how well he'd taken care of me in the shower. *Maybe don't go there.*

'He's not…' Evie's gaze darted to Vito. 'He's not keeping you there against your will?'

Vito tensed against my back. Was he expecting me to use the chance he'd given me against him? He still didn't really trust me, I realised.

So don't go getting ahead of yourself, Mia, and reading things into his behaviour that probably aren't there.

He'd made concessions I hadn't expected him to on the beach, but I'd made concessions too. It was still early days. And baby steps.

'No, he's not,' I said. 'I want to be here,' I added and meant it.

'And he wasn't angry you hadn't told him sooner?' Evie kept probing, watching me so carefully I suspected the strain of the last twenty-four hours was written all over my face.

We had never kept secrets from each other, not ever. But I knew however I'd got here, whatever had happened in the last twenty-four hours, I wasn't lying to her now when I replied.

'He wasn't too pleased,' I said. 'But he understands why I didn't tell him.'

Which was no small concession either. He seemed to have finally forgiven me for keeping his child a secret from him—despite what he had revealed about his past.

I also had to wonder now why he had come back when he had.

Had he been unable to forget me, too—after that night?

He'd taken a risk coming to London. I had no idea how much the authorities knew about his operations, but he'd used a secret airfield, flying in and out of the country without any of the usual checks. Exposing himself when he didn't have to, all just to see me. That had to count for something.

I felt him relax, his hand stroking my belly absently.

'Listen, Evie, you're going to have to contact the school and let them know I'm resigning. I've already arranged maternity cover for next term, but I don't want to leave them in the lurch.'

Evie's eyes widened. 'You're not coming back home?'

I had no idea what would happen in the long term. But I'd dealt with so much already in such a short period of time. I'd have to figure all that out in the next four months. I'd agreed to stay on Isla Donna, but there was so much else to work out. Good thing I was the queen of planning and practicalities.

'Not until after the baby is born,' I answered, anxiety knotting my belly again. 'Maybe you could come here for a visit,' I said tentatively.

I had no desire to pull Evie into Vito's world, but she seemed to have no qualms when her eyes lit up. 'Really, I'd love that. I miss you.'

'Use the savings account to pay my half of the rent, Eves,' I added, going into Mia the Manager mode and momentarily forgetting who was sitting behind me listening in to the conversation. 'I'll have to find another job once the baby is...'

'You will not work...and I will have one million euros transferred to your sister's account for her expenses.'

'Really?' Evie said at the exact same time I said, 'No you won't...'

I had no idea where Vito's money came from, and I didn't want to know. I was dealing with more than enough already. But there was one thing I was absolutely clear on.

'I don't want my sister implicated in whatever you do to afford all this...' I began.

'Stop.' He whispered in my ear, 'The money is clean. I spend a great deal of time and effort to ensure it. I am not an amateur, Mia.'

'That's not the point,' I said. 'I can't... What if someone died to make that money?' I started to babble, getting a bit frantic. This was why I did not want to think about this in my condition.

He kissed my nose. The look in his eyes was both patronising and amused, but the admiration there too made my heart stutter again.

'No one dies unless they threaten what is mine, Mia. It is not good for business. But your sister is mine now too, do you understand?'

'Yes, but...'

'I am?' Evie interrupted me, sounding more excited than concerned.

Good grief, this was getting totally out of hand.

Evie and I had never had the kind of money that meant we didn't have to constantly worry about how the next bill was going to be paid. We didn't have foreign holidays or expensive clothes. When our friends went out clubbing or to the pub, we stayed home and watched TV. I'd always thought Evie was okay with that. It was a struggle, but we'd never done anything illegal, if you didn't count forging our mum's signature on her cheques and claiming her benefits so we could stay together when she'd deserted us.

'We're not taking the money,' I tried again.

Vito tugged out his phone, typed something with his thumbs, then tucked the phone back into his pants pocket. 'It is done.'

'*Wh-what?* You can't just do that. You don't even know our account number…' I cried.

Then my objection was drowned out by Evie's squeal. 'Oh. My. God. Mia, I just got an email from a bank in Geneva… We're rich!'

She sounded so ecstatic, it only crucified me more.

'No we're not. We're not taking the…' I began again, but then Vito whipped the tablet he had given me to call Evie out of my hands, dumped me off his lap and stood up.

'Hey…give it back,' I cried, jumping up and dancing around trying to grab the tablet, which he simply lifted out of my reach while he talked to my sister.

'Enjoy the money,' he said to Evie, who had pound signs floating in her eyes now. 'I will arrange a visit for you here before the baby is born. And I will send men to keep watch on your apartment. You will not see them, but they will be there to keep you safe,' he added. 'If you need anything, contact me on the number I will send you, and use the code Sorella.'

'Wow, seriously? How cool,' Evie said, having gone to the dark side for a million euros.

Vito switched off the connection and dropped the tablet on the coffee table in front of me.

'I… I can't believe you just did that. What gives you the right to…'

'Stop. You know what gives me the right,' he said, dragging me towards him. Until my belly was pressed against his growing erection.

Seriously? He was hard again. How was that possible? And how come I was already melting at the thought of feeling him pounding me to orgasm again?

I slapped my hands against his chest.

'Just because I'm having your baby, you can't just…'

'She is my sister now too,' he broke in. The passion in his eyes disturbed me almost as much as the conviction. 'If she is not safe, you are not safe.'

'But you didn't have to give her all that money right now…' I tried.

'When did your mother abandon you…?' he asked, the abrupt change of subject and his sober expression confusing me even more.

Was that curiosity or pity? Or something much scarier… Tenderness. Compassion. Concern. The emotions I'd wanted to believe I had glimpsed before but knew I couldn't cope with now—when I felt so powerless and insecure about my growing feelings for him.

'How do you know that?' I asked, trying to delay this conversation until I had some sense of perspective again. Everything was moving too fast. I felt as if my whole life were being transformed in ways I had no control over. My common sense and my sense of right and wrong most of all.

He didn't even dignify that with a response, because we both knew Evie had let it slip.

I huffed out a breath. *Damn it*, why shouldn't I tell him? There was so much I wanted to know about him too. Maybe this was the opening I'd been waiting for. 'A long time ago… We were teenagers.'

'How old?' he asked.

I shrugged. 'I was fifteen, Evie nearly thirteen. But to be honest, Mum had clocked out of looking after us long before that. She wasn't what you'd call a natural at motherhood. And she was very young when she had us.'

'*Puttana.*' His brows lowered, the cold expression making me realise exactly what Vito's enemies would see if they dared to cross him. 'And your father, he was *never* there?'

'We never knew our fathers. They didn't stick around.'

'*They*?' he murmured, the frosty expression becoming turbulent.

I nodded, strangely embarrassed. Could our childhoods be any more pathetic, if even a mafia boss felt sorry for us? 'Strictly speaking, Evie and I are half sisters. My mum went through a phase of getting pregnant to try and attract a breadwinner. It backfired. *Twice.*'

He pressed his palm to my cheek. 'Your mamma sounds very selfish,' he murmured, the stormy expression softening with sympathy. 'I am sorry for this. My mother was selfish too, but she paid a heavy price.'

'How did she?' I asked, surprised and moved by his outraged reaction to what I'd confided about my childhood, but also eager to learn more about his. I had once assumed he'd led a charmed life, been spoilt and indulged as the son of a mafia boss. I knew now he hadn't been…

But I wanted to know so much more about what had made him choose this life so I could begin to understand it.

He frowned, and I knew I'd crossed a line I was not meant to cross. But when he just looked at me blankly, I made myself push.

'Why did she run away from your father?'

'Because she discovered herself pregnant with me… and my father was Salvatore Rocco, the boss of the Rocco Syndicate before me. She was scared for the safety of her unborn child.'

So Vito's father had been a mafia boss, too. Was it possible Vito had regrets about the life he'd been born into?

I soon realised I was way off the mark there, though, when his features hardened.

'She ran from the man who loved her and would have protected us, into the arms of a man who beat us both,' he sneered, his expression flat and unmoving. But the muscle in his jaw tightened, which meant he was struggling to control his reaction.

'This man *hurt* you? And your mother?' I asked, horrified, as I recalled the scars I had noticed on his body. So many scars, which I had dismissed as an integral part of the violent life he led. But what if they had been inflicted when he was still a child?

'I'm so sorry, Vito,' I murmured, devastated not just by the picture he had painted, but how wrong my assumptions had been about his past.

'Sorry means nothing, Mia,' he said, his tone brittle, his expression carefully devoid of emotion. 'She was sorry, too, for running to him—*uno poliziotto*.' He spat the word—which I assumed must mean policeman—as if it tasted foul. 'She thought he would protect her and me. But he was not a man. He was a monster. She killed herself to escape him.'

'Oh Vito…' I whispered, distraught at what he was revealing. That he still looked so unmoved only made the horror of his childhood more disturbing. Was this the real reason Vito had no respect for the law? Not because he profited from living outside it, but because a man who had been sworn to uphold it had hurt him and driven his mother to suicide? 'I can't even imagine how terrifying that must have been for you…' I whispered, tears sliding down my face now. To have no one? How had he survived?

He brushed a tear away with his thumb, the wary expression making my heart break even more.

'I do not require your pity, Mia,' he said. 'My father found me and showed me how to make him stop.' I had no idea what he meant by that, and I didn't want to guess.

'How old were you when your father rescued you?' I asked.

Was it any wonder he had grown up to be such a ruthless man if his formative years had been spent in hell? But did this also explain why he had been so determined to protect me and our baby? Because there had been no one to protect him?

He shrugged, the movement stiff. 'Ten, eleven. I do not know for sure. We did not celebrate birthdays in that house.'

I pressed a hand to my mouth to stop the gulping sob that wanted to come out, which I knew he wouldn't appreciate. My mother, however careless, however selfish and thoughtless and foolish, had never hurt us intentionally. And she'd never forgotten to celebrate our birthdays— even if it usually meant a last-minute dash to the corner shop to buy a kids' magazine with a toy attached. By the time she'd run off, she'd had a serious substance abuse problem, and while that didn't excuse her carelessness, it did explain it.

He ran his thumb across my collarbone where my pulse pounded, his eyes darkening.

'Why are you sad, Mia? This was long ago. And I made him pay.'

I nodded, aware he was uncomfortable with having told me so much. I didn't want him to regret it, though. So I forced a smile to my lips. 'I'm glad.'

His eyebrows rose, and he chuckled. But when his hands moved down to slide under the T-shirt he'd given me after our shower, I lifted my arms around his shoulders.

He pressed his lips to my neck, kissed the pulse point, even as emotion bombarded me.

I threaded my fingers into his hair and brought his mouth to mine, suddenly keen to lift the boulder off my chest that was making me think of him as a child, alone and brutalised. He wasn't that boy anymore, and I needed to remember that.

'Nothing matters now,' he said, his hands rising to cup my bottom under the shirt. 'Nothing but this,' he added.

I drew back to lift the T-shirt over my head, leaving me naked but for my panties.

His gaze became dark with need, his expression hard with hunger as he caressed my stomach, then cradled my breasts, thumbing the rigid tips into hard, aching peaks.

'Yes…' I sobbed, relishing the feel of those possessive hands on my body.

He scooped me into his arms and strode to the bed. Placing me on it, he reached behind him to tug off his own shirt, then dragged down his sweatpants. The heavy erection bounced free.

'On your knees, Mia,' he growled. 'I want your mouth on my cock.'

I did as he demanded, the heat building fast, knowing he was trying to control the situation by bringing our connection back to the sex, by dominating me again. But as I scrambled onto my knees, wrapped my fingers around his thick length and swirled my tongue over the tip, gathering the salty drops, I revelled in his shudder of response, no longer afraid of the emotions battering me.

This wasn't the only thing that mattered. He'd trusted me with information I suspected he rarely revealed to anyone. And that meant something.

Now I understood that his ruthlessness, his dominance, his arrogance and cynicism were all skills he'd needed to destroy a monster. How could I judge him for them when he'd used them to survive?

He plunged his fingers into my hair to press himself deep. I let the heat take me, envelop me, enjoying my ability to make him ache the way he made me ache.

He drew back moments later, positioning me on the bed to plunge to the hilt, stretching me wide, and forced me to another earth-shattering orgasm as he rode us both to completion…

Afterwards as I held him, my fingertips grazed the scars on his back.

So many scars.

Emotion swelled as it occurred to me his dominance was one of the things I had come to love about him—and not just in bed. Now I knew why. A part of me, that secret part of me who was still the abandoned little girl, had always wanted someone to protect me, even though

I'd learned to protect myself. That need had felt like a weakness I had to hide or ignore, but with Vito, it didn't feel like a weakness anymore…

Our connection had always been strong physically, and all the more overwhelming because of it. But why couldn't our connection be a part of something more, now we had the beginnings of trust?

So much had happened in the past five months—and especially in the past twenty-four hours. I needed time to process it all. But why not use the weeks ahead to nurture the bubble of hope now lodged under my breastbone?

The glimmering cloud of afterglow made anything seem possible.

Perhaps we'd both always needed someone to nurture us. To protect us. And if Vito could protect me, why shouldn't I protect him—from the darkness he had lived in for so long?

CHAPTER THIRTEEN

Vito

A month later

'WE HAVE DANTE. *He arrives tonight.*'

My muscles tightened as I read the text in Italian on my phone from Lorenzo, followed by a skull emoji. The text I had been waiting to receive for over six months.

I gazed out the bedroom window of the historic home I owned on Via Torino, Milan's luxury shopping street.

Aware of Mia in the bed behind me, my groin pulsed, reminding me of how she'd responded to me in the hours just before dawn, when I had woken her, hard and aching.

We'd spent the day yesterday shopping in a series of exclusive boutiques, her expression wary at first, her insistence she had never intended for me to spend so much money on her new wardrobe both captivating and amusing. After all, she had been badgering me for weeks to honour the promise I'd made to her a month ago to let her off the island.

I had wanted to forget the rash promise, had tried to make her forget it too. Because I hadn't wanted to trust her, and I had also enjoyed keeping her dressed in the clothes I'd had ordered for her online—which were more my style than hers, she'd pointed out several times. In other words, *revealing*. But eventually I had been forced to admit the truth. She had held up her side of the bargain, so I must hold up mine.

But always in the back of my mind had been the concern about Dante. What had disturbed me more, though, when I had whisked her to Milan in the jet and set about buying her whatever she desired—which turned out to be much less than I wished to give her—was admitting my fears for her safety were about a lot more than just the baby now.

Thank God my men had finally captured the son of a bitch. And were bringing him to Isla Donna as I had ordered.

I dialled Lorenzo's number. Keeping my voice low so as not to wake Mia, I spoke to him about what would happen next. But as I ended the call, the relief I wanted to feel didn't come. Instead dread settled like a block of ice in my stomach.

'Who's Dante?'

The sleepy whisper had me spinning round to find Mia standing behind me draped in a sheet, her round belly more pronounced now than a month ago. Devoid of makeup, her heart-shaped face was still groggy with sleep and her hair even wilder than usual from our early-morning lovemaking.

Even though we had fucked less than an hour ago, I felt the familiar wave of arousal sink into my groin… and pound in the pyjama pants I had put on when I'd received the text.

When was I going to tire of her, and why did she captivate me so? Was it simply that she carried my child, as

I had tried so hard to convince myself since bringing her to Isla Donna? Or was it her live wire responses, her silent strength, that intoxicating combination of determination and pragmatism and innocence which had made me start to trust her, to become addicted to her presence, more than I should?

I clicked off the phone and dropped it into the pocket of my pants, then clasped her neck and drew her towards me to press my face into the soft mass of her hair. I inhaled the intoxicating aroma which clung to her, that unique perfume of spring flowers and sex.

'Nobody,' I murmured—angry that Dante had intruded onto our time here together.

We would have to return to Isla Donna a day early. Perhaps I should leave her in Milan, I thought as I pulled the sheet aside to cup her naked bottom. It would be safer for her here while I concluded my business with Dante.

But a part of me knew, as she let out a sob against my neck, signaling her arousal, that it wasn't just her safety I wanted to insure. I also wished to keep her away from the darkest side of my life.

Dante was a dead man, and once he was gone, the threat he posed would be dead too. But while I'd been waiting for him to leave the Malvini estate near Sicily, I had spent the past weeks indulging myself with Mia, taking a time-out on Isla Donna—allowing myself to be distracted, enjoying my time with her.

Mia's sweetness, her artlessness, our conversations about the baby and her sister's impending visit, and her dogged attempts to learn more about my past—which I had deflected—had been as captivating as her eagerness to explore our insane chemistry. She had been a delightful distraction, an addiction, an escape even from the demands of the syndicate—and the knowledge of what needed to happen next.

But news of Dante's capture meant I would have to return to reality today, confront my brother and then end him myself.

He deserved that much.

But right now, I did not want to think about him. Or what he was forcing me to do.

I threaded my fingers through her hair, loving the feel of the silky softness, and pressed a kiss to the pulse point in her neck. She shuddered, but as I clasped her to me, to grind my already lengthening cock against her soft curves, planning to get lost in her again, she flattened her palms on my chest and pushed me gently back.

'I know Dante's not nobody, Vito,' she said softly, her chin firm.

I stiffened, the sound of his name on her lips making the emotions I did not want to confront—not just about my brother, but also about her—surge.

'*How* do you know this?' I demanded, regretting the sharp tone when she flinched. I realised I had said too much because her mossy-green eyes became shadowed with concern.

'The women talk about him sometimes when they think I don't understand,' she added, making me curse the fact I had allowed her to befriend the other women on the island while I worked during the day. But I had enjoyed watching her make friends on Isla Donna as she taught them English and they taught her Italian. I regretted that, too, when she continued. 'And you looked so troubled when you were talking about him on the phone just now with Lorenzo. Who is he? Why is he being brought to Isla

Donna? Is he the man who tried to kill you that night? I want to know who…'

'No, you don't, Mia,' I interrupted her, pressing my finger to her lips to silence her, my stomach starting to churn. 'He is not your concern.'

She grasped my finger and dragged it away, still staring at me with that crippling concern in her eyes. 'Of course he is, if he wants to kill you,' she said. But the fierceness in her gaze only troubled me more.

I had told her once she could not save me when I did not want to be saved. But why did I still find her refusal to obey me as enchanting as it was frustrating?

'He doesn't *want* to kill me any more than I *want* to kill him.' I ground out the words, forced to admit the truth. 'But he will keep trying until he gets what he believes is rightfully his.'

As a boy, my younger half brother, Dante, had been reckless, impulsive and dangerously charismatic—but he had also hero-worshipped me. Even though, when I had first arrived on Isla Donna scared and alone and traumatised, I had taken his place, declared as the heir because I was my father's first-born child and his only legitimate son.

My father had always been a hard man, but why, when he had valued family so much, had he treated his own flesh and blood so cruelly? Discarding Dante and his mother less than a year later, when he tired of Angelica Malvini's charms.

After my father's death two years ago, the prospect of joining forces with Dante and the Malvini family had seemed to make more sense than prolonging a feud which could bleed into generations.

But all thoughts of a compromise had been lost six

months ago in Naples, when I had seen the bullets fly across the bed so close to Mia's head. Had I instinctively known my son was already growing inside her, that I must protect her at all costs? As I stared at her now, her gaze glowing with compassion, I finally admitted to myself my attachment to her wasn't just about the baby anymore. If it had ever been… Something had happened between us that night which had changed me even then. And it had got progressively worse since I had brought her to Isla Donna.

I trusted her now more than I had ever trusted anyone. She hadn't lied about accepting her place was here with me. She had even begun to build a life in the compound. I had enjoyed seeing her blossom, seeing her start to belong, but I could not allow her to make me weak.

'Why does he think he should have a share of the syndicate?' she asked, clearly believing my silence was an opportunity to push for information.

'Because he is my father's son too,' I said, the truth bitter on my tongue.

'He's… Dante's your *brother*?' she whispered, recoiling in horror at the implication.

I nodded. 'We will return to Isla Donna today, and then tonight, this will be over,' I said flatly, determined not to let her shocked reaction matter.

She needed to know how this worked. She needed to understand that there could be no compromise. Not in my world. Or Dante's. He understood there was a price to be paid for threatening my men, my businesses, for threatening me and my woman and my child, even if Mia did not.

She shuddered as the impact of my words hit her.

'But you can't kill him, Vito. You said yourself you don't want to. And he's your brother… There must be another way.' She swallowed, her gaze rivetted to my face now. 'I... I'm falling in love with you Vito,' she said. The quiet words sliced through me.

But I steeled myself against the sudden rush of longing for it to be true.

What the hell was happening to me? I couldn't need her love. I didn't want it. That was not what this was about. She was mine now, and I had realised in the past weeks I might never be able to let her go.

In just a few weeks, she had become an integral part of my existence. The time we had spent together was the lightest of my life. I had come to crave the way she challenged me, the way she could be both practical and playful, the way she could turn me on to the point of madness at one moment and yet bring me peace the next. Most nights now, I slept soundly as I held her, her steady breathing keeping the old nightmares at bay and making the danger that had always haunted my life seem distant.

But that did not mean I was going to start believing in fairy tales.

'If you kill Dante,' she said, her distress written all over her expressive face, 'and you don't have to, how will you ever live with yourself...'

I grasped her arms, yanked her onto her toes, the searing jealousy helping me to bury all those needs I didn't want to feel. 'Why do you care so much about him?'

'It's not *him* I care about. It's *you*,' she said, her tone direct and unafraid. 'And what this might do to you. He's your brother, Vito, and it's obvious you're conflicted about this.'

I dropped her arms as if I'd been burned. How could she know that? Did trusting her, wanting her too much, allow her to see into my soul?

I let out a harsh laugh, the raw sound scraping my throat.

'He will not be my brother for much longer,' I said, knowing the time had come to kill the naïveté I had always found so captivating. I had believed I should shield Mia from the darkest aspects of my life. But why should I when she was a part of my world now?

I gripped her chin and lifted her gaze to mine so she could see what lurked inside me.

'This is who I am, Mia. And I am not ashamed of that. Love me if you want, but don't seek to change me.'

There could be no soft feelings, no sentimental attachments, not for a man like me, or it would leave me vulnerable. As I had once been as a boy. Before my father had found me—and shown me the only way to survive in this world was to be ruthless, to remain invulnerable, to be ready to kill your demons, whoever they were.

'Please, Vito, don't do this. For me.' She covered her belly where our baby grew. 'For us. The feud might never end. And it will hurt you, too.'

Tears shimmered in her eyes. I stared at her. Did she have any idea what she was asking of me? Of course she didn't. But if she loved me, it was time she learned to accept all of me.

'That's where you're wrong,' I countered. 'I killed my first man when I was ten years old, and I would do it again in a heartbeat. The man you think you are in love with died a long time ago, because I killed him when he was still a boy.'

A cloud passed over the sun as tears dripped over her lids to roll down her cheeks. But this time, I refused to scoop them up or pander to the weakness in me which made me want to stop them.

I expected her to be horrified, but to my shock, she pressed her palm to my cheek, the acceptance in her gaze staggering me. But also making that hollow empty ache in my stomach swell and the lump of dread become sharp and jagged.

'Who did you kill?' she asked.

'My stepfather, Andrea Grimaldi.' I spat the words out.

I could still feel the weight of the gun my father had pressed into my palm, the heavy silencer making it difficult for my small hands to keep the barrel level. I could still hear his toneless whisper echoing in my head.

'Take the revenge you deserve, for your mother, for yourself.'

I could still see my stepfather's panicked expression, the sweat streaking through the blood from the beating my father's men had already administered. But the smell of his fear always changed into my mother's fear and mine through all the years of my childhood. So when I heard the quiet pop as I pressed the trigger and the muffled thump as his big body hit the ground, his lifeless eyes staring back at me as the metallic smell of blood mixed with the damp scent of dirty concrete, I refused to be ashamed of what that boy had done.

'The man who beat you and your mother?' she whispered, drawing me out of memory. I tensed but could not deny it. 'I would never judge you for that, Vito.'

'*Really*?' I sneered. I grasped her hand to pull it away from my face. I didn't need her forgiveness. I didn't want it. 'He was unarmed, and I shot him through the heart. And I will never regret it.'

'I don't care. You said yourself he was a monster, and you were just a child, a *brutalised* child,' she replied, her fierce defence of that terrified boy only disturbing me more. 'Please don't shut me out, Vito,' she said, but when she reached for me again, I grabbed her wrist to stop her touching me, to stop her caressing me.

Dragging her into my arms, I ground my lips against hers, to silence her, to stop her pleas, to control that empty ache inside me that I had never quite been able to kill, no matter how many times I made her come.

'This is all I want from you,' I said, stripping the sheet from her.

I palmed her naked curves, kneading the soft flesh, pinching those responsive nipples until they hardened. But instead of stopping me, instead of being shocked or horrified, she moaned into my mouth—and the hunger that never ceased consumed me again.

I grasped her arm and dragged her to the bed, then knelt between her legs. I clasped her hips, brought her to my mouth to devour the slick folds already wet for me. All I wanted now was to drive her into a frenzy—and finally regain the control I had lost weeks ago.

She bucked beneath me, sinking her fingers into my hair. I caressed the mound of her pregnancy—brutally aware of the changes my child had brought to her body— as I feasted on the plump nub of her clitoris and worked her tight flesh with my fingers.

She sobbed, panted, then cried out my name, contracting around my fingers as the brutal orgasm powered through her.

'This is all I need from you,' I said as I rose above her, willing it to be true, my voice raw with desperation.

She didn't object as I flipped her over, dragged her to her knees, then positioned her on all fours so I could drive into her from behind. I plunged deep in one heavy thrust—determined to claim her, conquer her and silence my fears.

But as she tightened around me, her staggered sobs matching my brutal grunts, her eager acceptance of me had the last of my control shattering. I rode the devastating wave, digging in, rocking back, again and again, ruthlessly caressing the place deep inside her I knew would trigger another orgasm.

She massaged my aching length, her body responding to me with the same fierce passion as always, holding nothing back.

I kept pounding until the climax overwhelmed me, too. But as I rolled off her, drenched in sweat, all I could hear was my thundering heart, and all I could feel was the hollow, empty ache in my gut expanding.

Because the weakness for her, the need for something more and the fear of what that need could cost me, was still there.

Instead of holding her the way I usually would, I dragged myself from the bed. She sat up, clasping the sheet to her nakedness with shaking fingers, but I didn't look at her as I found my pants and put them back on.

'I must return to Isla Donna,' I said, keeping my voice flat, my tone cold, determined to destroy the fear still churning in my gut. 'I will have my men escort you back later today.'

I ground the words out to diminish her, to make her realise she would never have more from me than this.

'Please, Vito, this isn't who you are…' she began, forcing me to look at her.

I leaned down and grasped her chin.

'This is exactly who I am. You think because I like to fuck you…' I let my gaze roam to her belly '…because you will have my child, that I will let you weaken me? I won't. Tonight, once Dante is dead, once I have *killed* him…' I reiterated, lifting her chin, forcing myself to ignore the tearing sensation in my chest as tears leaked out of her eyes and she shuddered under my touch, 'I will expect you to be in my bed, waiting for me. And we both know you will not deny me.'

But when I released my hold on her, instead of cowering as I had hoped, instead of looking broken or beaten, she stared at me, that damn compassion still shining in her eyes and annihilating me.

'I fell in love with you, Vito, knowing how ruthless you can be, and how violent,' she said. 'I'm not that clueless girl you got pregnant six months ago. I had to be strong and smart and pragmatic to survive my childhood, just like you did. And I accepted that loving you meant accepting the darkness in you. But I've also seen the light now too. The way you hold me so you can sleep. The way you caress my stomach because of the connection you feel to our child. The way you are so determined to protect me, no matter what it costs.' She lifted her head, her expression brave and bold and unbowed. 'And for that reason, I'll still love you even if you kill him. But only if you do it because you believe you must to protect our baby.' She bit into her lip to control the quiver of emotion which was already crucifying me, the jagged boulder growing in my throat. 'But what I won't do is let you bully me, or watch you destroy what's left of your soul, just because you're too scared to admit you have feelings for me, too.'

'What the fuck are you even talking about now?' I yelled as panic consumed me.

The shout echoed around the bedroom, my insides churning with the fear I wanted so desperately to deny.

That she was right about me, and I wrong. That I *could* love her, that I already did.

She didn't even flinch, crucifying me even more. 'I think you know…' she said with a bravery that destroyed me.

I turned and walked away, storming through the house. I got dressed, threw a few things into a bag, then headed down the stairs into the courtyard where my men were waiting. But as I climbed into the car which would take me to the airport, the storm of emotions she had caused still raged inside me—not just fear and fury and panic now, but by far the most terrifying emotion of all…*hope*.

Mia

I was still shaking, still struggling to control my tears when Lorenzo arrived at the Milan house a few hours later, sent to escort me back to Isla Donna.

I kept my spine ramrod straight, feeling sick to my stomach when the bags and boxes of our shopping spree the day before were loaded into the car which had arrived to take me to the airport.

Had it really only been yesterday that everything had seemed so possible, so light between Vito and me? His lavish generosity during the day-long shopping spree, his smiles every time I tried to save him money—which only seemed to make him insist on spending even more—his enthusiasm as he showed me the city, his attention to my needs and the fact he'd upheld his part of our bargain to let me off the island even though I knew he was still concerned about my safety, had made me feel cherished and precious to him and seen…

When he'd woken me just before dawn, his callused hands stroking my stomach, I'd turned over, eager to make love to him again, to confirm what I already knew.

I'd seen so much of who Vito was since he'd brought me to Isla Donna. Not just the darkness inside him, but also the light which I was pretty sure he had never intended for me to see, but which he also hadn't been able to hide. And it had given me hope for so much more, not just yesterday, but even before that.

He *was* ruthless, and I knew he wouldn't hesitate to kill when he considered it necessary…and I'd had to accept that about him.

But each time he touched me with such tenderness, each time he held me securely, each time I saw his eyes glaze with awe when he caressed my bump or heat with approval when I challenged him or burn with passion when he thrust heavily inside me, I saw that other man. The man he was to me. So protective, so possessive, but also vulnerable in ways I suspected he hadn't been since he was a little boy, beaten by the man I now knew he had eventually killed.

And over the past weeks, I'd fallen hopelessly in love with both those men.

But when the helicopter finally arrived back at the villa on Isla Donna, I had been told Vito was locked in his study and had no wish to see me until later tonight.

Dismissed, I rushed to the bedroom, locked the bathroom door and let the tears come, unable to hold back the well of fear any longer, the tearing pain caused by our argument… I stuffed a fist into my mouth because I didn't want anyone to hear the wracking sobs.

Until this morning, I'd convinced myself he had struggled not because he *couldn't* love me, but because he was terrified to be that vulnerable. I knew he saw love as a weakness, and it would be a major battle to prove to him it could also be a strength.

But as I'd sat alone in the Milan house and on the journey back to Isla Donna, I'd had far too much time to examine and dissect every part of our argument, and the way he'd treated me, and all the awful things he'd said to me in that scathing tone… And it had made me wonder if I'd been a naive fool to ever hope for more from him.

What if this was a struggle neither of us could win? What if he could never allow himself to love me too? I'd accepted that it would take time to break down all the barriers he'd had to erect since his childhood to keep himself and the people who relied on him safe. But what if I'd sold my soul to the devil, and he really didn't want more from me than someone to warm his bed and give birth to his son?

I'd seen the fury in Vito's eyes when I'd mentioned Dante's name, seen the anxiety and the conflicting emotions battering him when I'd woken up and watched him speaking to Lorenzo that morning.

I knew from the older women I'd befriended on the island that Vito and Dante had been close as children for a year before his father had kicked the boy and his mother out of the compound. But I hadn't known they were also brothers.

Ultimately, though, this wasn't about Dante. I didn't know the guy. And I would happily shoot him myself if he ever threatened me or Vito or our child again the way he had in Naples. Because I was much tougher and more resilient than I had been then.

All I'd wanted Vito to know was that there was a way out—if he wanted to take it. That killing Dante didn't have to be inevitable, if it meant destroying a part of his own soul. But his furious reaction to my suggestion had told me exactly how hard it was going to be for him to ever let me in.

When the gulping sobs finally passed, I pushed myself off the floor and took a shower. I felt weak and groggy and still scared. Because I knew, whatever he did about Dante tonight, I'd revealed my feelings. If he talked to me again or made love to me the way he had this morning, with that furious look in his eyes, it would make me doubt myself even more. And every time he pushed me away, every time he used sex to control his feelings, to control me, it would chip away another little piece of my heart and my self-respect and my hope.

And if he killed Dante just to protect himself from feeling anything at all…if he treated me again with the contempt he had this morning, how did either of us come back from that?

I'd wanted to prove to him I was strong, that I wasn't afraid of loving him, that the passion we shared, the desire to protect each other, went both ways.

But what if I wasn't tough enough to ever punch through the walls he'd built around his heart? What if hope wasn't enough to weather the pain he could cause me while I waited for him to let me in? And how would I ever survive being a mafia don's woman, changing my own life so fundamentally to love him, if he could never ever offer me the same love in return?

CHAPTER FOURTEEN

Vito

'Leave us,' I ordered the guards as I stepped into the dank cell where Dante had been chained.

He'd arrived on the island that morning only a few hours before me, but I could see my men had not been idle in the hours while I had stewed in my office at the villa, cursing Mia, before crossing the island to finish this.

My stomach contracted, the riot of emotions Mia had caused no longer something I could control as I stared at the man I had loved as a boy.

His shirt was torn and bloody, the welts on his back and shoulders visible even in the shadows. He was slumped against the wall, his forehead resting against the cold stone, his wrists manacled, and his arms chained above his head in an uncomfortable position. Some of the injuries might have been caused when he was taken in a café in Avellino, a small town near Naples—because the bastard was just that audacious. But not all of them.

I had not sanctioned the beating, but neither had I forbidden it, and I could not blame my men for wanting revenge. While no one had died during the attack in Naples, several of them had sustained injuries, some of them severe, mine included.

He didn't turn to look at me as I stepped into the cell, but his shoulders tensed. I was glad he was not unconscious. He deserved to know why he would die, I told myself, even as the pit in my stomach—the pit I had struggled to close ever since listening to Mia's pleas—continued to widen.

Do not listen to her. She has no place in your heart. No one does. No one can.

'Give me the keys,' I murmured as the last guard walked past me to exit the cell.

The guard hesitated before handing them over. 'Be careful of him, *padrino*. He is strong, and he does not know when he is beaten.'

'So nothing has changed then,' I muttered.

The wry comment echoed in the airless room, the scent of blood and dirt suffocating. I could not deny the swell of admiration that Dante had fought like hell to defy his fate. But then the pride mixed with the anger and resentment which had driven me to this point, but also the fear and regret Mia had stirred that morning when she had begged me to reconsider ending Dante's life. Emotions which had infuriated me then, but pushed against my chest now like a heavy weight I could not lift.

'Please, Vito, don't do this. For me. For us. The feud might never end. And it will hurt you, too.'

Damn it, why couldn't I get those words out of my head?

The gun I had holstered under my arm felt so much heavier than usual. But instead of drawing it and taking the shot I had been envisioning for months now, I found myself lifting a chair and slamming it down beside my brother's slumped body. The thought of Mia's pleas and the deep compassion in her eyes started to crush my ribs and made it hard for me to breathe.

I sat down, folding my arms over the back of the chair as the emotions I had been afraid of, the emotions she had stirred, drained the last of the anger I had felt towards this man for so long…

Again, Dante didn't raise his head, but I saw tension ripple down his spine, his back a mass of purpling bruises.

Suddenly I was drawn back to the day when I had seen him last…not a man then but just a child, fierce and loyal and confused. I could hear the sound of that boy's angry tears, the squeal of the mongrel puppy he had nurtured. The brutal crack of my father's hand across his face as Dante had tried to defend his treasured pet. And the hollow pop of the gun my father had used to kill it.

I huffed out a breath. And let the emotion claim me this time.

I didn't just want Mia. I needed her. I loved her. But I was terrified of admitting it to myself because of everything that had happened on that terrible day, when I had let my father do something unforgiveable to Dante, to his dog, and had done nothing to help him.

Could I save him now, save us both, by finding another way? The weight eased, the heavy burden of guilt I hadn't even realised had been crushing me for a very long time lifting at last.

Fuck it. Mia *had* been right.

I needed Mia. I wanted her. Why shouldn't I have her? If I showed Dante mercy, would it make me worthy of her, would it prove I deserved her? All of her. Not just her body. Not just her loyalty, but also her love?

'If you're going to fucking kill me, just do it.' Dante's

slurred voice pulled me out of my thoughts. Defiant, insolent and full of the same rage which had once filled me.

'Look at me, you coward,' I snarled, letting my anger towards him show. I was damned if I was going to make this easy for him.

But when he raised his head, and I saw his face up close for the first time in twenty years, the compassion I'd tried so hard to deny welled up inside me.

One eye was swollen shut, but the other was the same sky blue as my own. Would my son inherit that colour too? If he did, and I murdered Dante now, how would I look at my son and not see Dante again?

His face was swollen, fresh blood smeared across his lips, and new bruises were purpling on his jaw. But beneath the swelling, I could see so much of what I saw in the mirror each morning—and also so much of that boy who had followed me around on this island, chatting away aimlessly about anything and everything, that mongrel puppy trailing behind him, until I hadn't been able to stop myself from bonding with him. From loving him like a brother.

Funny to think we had always looked more like full brothers than half brothers, the only real difference being his darker skin—a result of his mother's Moroccan grandfather, I suspected.

'What the fuck are you looking at?' he sneered, goading me now.

Yeah, he was still a hothead, still a threat. But I'd be damned if I'd allow him to destroy what I had with Mia.

I sighed.

I could not be soft on Dante. He had done something unforgiveable, and he deserved to be punished. And if I was not going to kill him, I also knew I could not set him free. Until I knew he would no longer be a threat, because now I had so much more to protect.

So I would have to find another way to end this blood feud my father had started. The man who had chosen to discard one son while saving another.

I got off the chair, kicked it away, and then knelt beside him and gripped his hair.

He hissed, his swollen jaw clenching as I yanked his head back to glare into his eyes.

'If you were anyone but my brother, you would be dead already,' I said, and meant it.

But something flickered in his eyes, something that looked like shock before he could mask it… And suddenly I wondered, had he really meant to kill me that night?

No one had died. *Why* had no one died? I'd thought at the time it was because our firepower was greater, but what the guard had said came back to me now.

'He does not know when he is beaten.'

And I could still remember the eight-year-old boy who had kept punching, kept fighting, even as my father had slapped him down over and over again before killing his dog.

Dante would have fought to the death to kill me that night if that had been his intention.

'So, we're brothers again, are we?' he sneered, but I heard the weariness and pain he was trying so hard to hide, as well as the anger.

'We never stopped being brothers, *idiota*,' I murmured.

I let go of his hair, satisfied I had got my point across when his head hit the wall with a solid thunk.

He was cursing me, telling me to kill him and get it over with, as I walked out of the cell without looking back and locked the door.

Figuring out what to do with that dumb bastard was a problem for another day. He could rot in this hole for a long while for all I cared. It would give him time to consider his actions. But I had something much bigger and more important to figure out first.

I bounded up the stairs, suddenly desperate to see Mia, to hold her, to take the devastated look out of her eyes, the terrible hope making my heart pound and my ribs hurt.

I was a bad man, a bad person, and I would still do bad things, but tonight I had to find a way to prove to her she would always be an oasis of good in me. That I wanted the lightness she had brought into my life. That I loved it—and her.

And I had a bad feeling that meant, for the first time in my life, I was going to have to beg.

When I got to our bedroom, though, and she wasn't waiting for me as I had demanded, I had to clamp down on the swift surge of fury…and panic.

As I searched the villa's rooms unable to find her, the panic turned to fear. But as I raced back through the house, ready to initiate a search of the island, I spotted a moonlit figure in the cove below.

Mia.

I choked down the panic, but the fear remained as I watched her step into the water. Visceral dread washed through me. And for a moment I was rooted to the stone terrace, unable to move, unable to think.

Was she intending to kill herself to escape me? The way my mother had, to escape him…?

Had I done that to her? Had I caused this by my actions? Of course I had. Because I had made her feel she was worthless, that she meant nothing to me, in order to protect myself.

Adrenaline coursed through my body on a wave of pain, propelling me to the steps to stop her. But as I charged down them two at a time, a wave of terror and regret rose up my throat to choke me.

Mia

'*Fermati*, Mia!'

I swung round to see Vito running across the sand towards me. The way he had so many weeks ago now.

I'd come to the cove to feel the sea on my body, to cool the burning pain in my heart and to figure out how to go on from here. I had watched Vito leave the villa an hour ago from our bedroom window on a motorbike, a gun holstered under his arm.

But when he reached me this time, instead of the fury from weeks ago or the cold resentment from this morning, all I saw was fear.

He sank to his knees in front of me and wrapped his arms around my legs, rubbing his cheek against my belly, holding me so tightly I could feel his stubble through the cotton negligée.

'Do not do it. Do not leave me. I didn't kill him. I couldn't.'

'Vito!' I thrust shaking fingers into his hair to pull his head back, hearing the anguish in his voice even as my heart lifted and rammed my chest wall.

His blue eyes looked pale in the moonlight, and wild with grief.

'Y-you didn't kill your brother?'

He shook his head. 'The men have beaten him, which

is what he deserves,' he said with venom. But then he grasped my bottom to press his face even harder into my belly, his voice muffled when he added, 'And he will remain a prisoner here—until I decide what to do with him. But no, I did not kill him.'

I stroked his hair, the short, silky spikes damp with sweat, my heart so light it felt as if it might fly off into the starry night above us. The night which had seemed so dark and forbidding only moments before.

'I'm glad,' I murmured, then swallowed down the searing hope, not wanting to let it overwhelm me too soon. 'But why did you spare him?'

He let out a heavy sigh, then drew his head back so he could look into my eyes.

'Because you were right,' he said, his voice a growl of regret. 'Dante was the only person I ever truly cared for, until I met you… He was my brother, and I made myself hate him. I thought this made me strong, invincible. But then you came into my life and made me want things I did not understand.' He blinked, his own eyes shimmering with tears now too, tears I knew he would never shed for anyone but me. 'I thought if I had feelings for you, they would make me weak. I thought I could control them if I controlled you. But then I fell in love with you anyway… And I could not control any of it.'

I jolted, shocked by the pain in his voice and the joy surging into my heart.

'And it terrified you?' I murmured, but I already knew the answer to that. Because our love had terrified me too.

He nodded, then climbed to his feet to draw me against him, to press his lips to my hair. He held me so tightly, I could feel his voice reverberating in his sternum as he spoke.

'Yes, it did. *You* terrify me, Mia. Your bravery, your trust, your passion. I have been scared to feel anything for so long. I never wanted to feel this way about anyone. But with you, I did not ever have a choice. This is ironic, no?' He huffed. 'When you once accused me of taking your choices away from you.'

I laughed. I couldn't help it, he sounded so annoyed and dumbfounded.

He clasped my cheeks to tilt my head back and push my hair away from my face. He brushed his thumbs over my tear-streaked cheeks as the emotion of his declaration blindsided me again.

'Don't cry, Mia. It destroys me,' he said, pressing his lips to my cheeks to kiss away the tears, even though they were happy tears now. 'I'm so sorry for what I said, for what I did this morning. For treating you like a whore when you will always be a goddess to me. You must forgive me.'

I let out a jagged sigh, moved by the genuine agony in his voice—and the tenderness I knew he would only ever let me see.

I cradled his cheek, felt his jaw tense, and let my heart show in my eyes. 'Okay, I'll forgive you, but I think there has to be payback,' I said, trying for flirtatious but getting overjoyed instead.

A sensual smile spread across his lips. Then he swung me into his arms to march towards the beach sofa he'd had installed weeks ago, after the first time we'd made love here on the sand.

'Name it,' he said. 'Whatever penance you decide, I will pay it, and gladly.'

I grasped his cheek to draw his gaze to mine, giddy with love at the thought of this dominant, powerful man trusting our love enough to hand over his precious control to me.

'I think perhaps you should be my sex slave for the rest of the night,' I teased, my heart light with joy.

Especially when he frowned but said, 'Consider it done.'

Several mind-blowing orgasms later, during which he had already forgotten his promise not to dominate, he told me again he had given me his heart…and begged me to forgive him.

As I lay draped over him in the moonlight, his arms around me, the afterglow shimmering through my body, both of us naked and exhausted, I listened to the lap of the water while the sweat dried on my skin.

And I knew, whatever happened next in the dangerous world in which I now lived, I would never want to be anywhere else, because my heart would always be safe with him.

EPILOGUE

Mia

Two months later

'DON'T YOU EVER feel guilty, Mia?'

I shifted round on the lounger to find Evie staring at me wide-eyed. This was her second visit to Isla Donna since I had come to live on Vito's island… Vito had made a huge fuss over her, and she'd loved being here, I knew that. He'd also spoilt us both rotten this week with another trip to Milan on the jet, to purchase a wardrobe for both Evie and me this time as a belated Christmas present.

I ran my open palms over my now enormous belly. It was late January already, but we'd had a rare chance to use the pool today vecause of an unseasonably warm spell.

My new wardrobe had been designer maternity clothes—which I had tried to explain to Vito weren't necessary, because the baby was due in less than a month. But I'd eventually given in to the trip because I had known Evie would adore it, especially after having to spend her first Christmas alone in London, and I'd also known that Vito was still a little unsure of my love for him. Apparently allowing him to buy me and my sister a load of unnecessary clothes helped put his mind at rest, so who was I or Evie to complain?

'Guilty about what?' I asked, concerned that Evie was finally going to ask questions about Vito's businesses. I had never questioned him about what he did for a living. It was part of our unspoken agreement. An agreement I'd signed up to by loving him. And the rewards had been, well…*incredible*. Not in monetary things, not really. As much as I had come to love living on Isla Donna, it was him I wanted, not his wealth. It was that feeling he gave me of being cherished and adored, the knowledge that he would do anything to protect me and the baby.

Vito was still an unreconstructed alpha male, which meant he still insisted on bossing me around every chance he got. And while his dominance worked in bed—because it was seriously hot—whenever he got too bossy out of it, I now knew I simply had to stand up to him. And he could be reasoned with. Because he loved me and wanted me to be happy. And when he pressed and I pushed back, it also usually led to lots of hot makeup sex. So there was that…

Although in the past couple of weeks, as I had become increasingly enormous, he had become much more tender in bed and out of it. The look of awe in his eyes as he stroked my belly at night after we'd made love, or in the mornings when the baby was usually super active, had only added to the deep sense of belonging I felt in his arms.

He was the one who had surprised me a week ago with a visit from Evie. I'd only discovered this morning that he had brought her here because he was concerned the baby might arrive early, and he had wanted me to have her support during the birth. His thoughtfulness had surprised me, not because he didn't constantly show his compassionate side to me, but because I knew he was still struggling with the problem of how to deal with Dante, and the island had been in lockdown as a result.

But as I steeled myself to deal with any difficult questions from Evie, her face lit up with what could only be described as excitement.

'Guilty that we're living like queens,' Evie said, her voice hushed but animated. 'While Vito has his brother locked up in a dungeon here…?'

I manoeuvred myself up so I was sitting on the lounger and snuggled into the warm swimming robe I'd brought down to the pool, a chill running through my body. 'How do you know about Dante, Evie?' I asked, not liking the sparkle in her eyes. Evie had always loved drama, so it didn't surprise me that she'd romanticise this situation. But Vito would be unhappy that she even knew about Dante being here. No one was supposed to know of his whereabouts.

'I was on my morning run yesterday on the other side of the island, Mia, and I saw him. Lorenzo was with him, and some of the other men. Did you know they've been beating him?'

I knew that Vito had ordered the beatings to stop, I would have to tell him that may not have happened. But that wasn't the point, as far as Evie was concerned.

'Don't go there again, Evie. You're not supposed to be on that side of the island.' Something my inquisitive little sister had been warned about before. 'How did you know who he was?' I asked. If someone had leaked the information, Vito would be furious.

'Oh, come on, Mia, it's obvious if you look at him. They're so alike. He's even more handsome than Vito.'

I'd never seen Dante. Vito had insisted I did not need

to know what was going on in the negotiations with the Malvinis, and I'd respected that. He'd promised me he wouldn't kill his brother, and I knew he wouldn't break that promise, so that was enough for me. It wasn't my business what happened to his brother while he was held prisoner here.

But the dreamy look in Evie's eyes was totally my business.

I grasped Evie's hand and held on to it. 'Listen to me, Evie. Dante may be handsome, but he is incredibly dangerous. He has a grudge against Vito and the Rocco Syndicate. It was him and his mob who shot at us on our first night together. Don't go near him again. Do you understand?'

Evie nodded, her face pale. 'It was him?' She looked horrified. '*He* was the one who tried to kill you both?'

'Yes, he was,' I said, even though I knew it wasn't entirely true.

Vito had assured me Dante hadn't actually been attempting to kill us that night. He had become convinced in the arguments he'd had with Dante while he was captive here, that the nighttime raid on the estate in Naples, the night we'd made our baby, had been a show of strength, a warning that had gone wrong. But I decided it was better to let Evie believe the worst.

I had no doubt at all Dante Malvini was a ruthless killer. So it made sense for me to make sure Evie realised how dangerous he was.

I squeezed her fingers. 'This isn't a game, Evie. Or a movie. This is my real life now. I trust Vito to keep us both safe, or I wouldn't let him bring you here. But you have a responsibility too, not to do anything to jeopardise your own safety.'

I knew how much Vito loved me now, because he showed me every single day. All those long looks, the sparkle of approval as well as arousal that was always there in his eyes, that told me I fascinated and intrigued and captivated him. The way he adored it when I challenged him or said something witty or caustic. I knew he admired my strength and my determination, as well as my compassion and empathy, things he had had far too little of in his life.

But I also knew that what we had, what we were building together, was pretty unique, especially in his world. He'd made allowances for me, had softened his desire to be in total control of everything and everyone to make space for my choices, my freedom. He'd also made allowances for Evie, trusting her the way he trusted me, just because she was my sister. And no way on earth was I going to throw that back in his face by putting either one of us…or my baby…in unnecessary danger.

I could see I had got my message across when Evie squeezed my fingers back, her face red.

'Of course, Mia. I get it. And I'm sorry. I guess there's a bit too much of Mum in me sometimes…' She grinned that cheeky reckless grin I had always adored, despite the fact it had got us both into trouble more than once. 'And he is super good-looking!'

'Stop,' I groaned.

'Who is super good-looking?'

We both swung round to see Vito walking across the pool terrace towards us. He'd been gone for several days on a business trip to Rome. My heart leapt into my throat at the sight of him again… I'd missed him so much.

The throb of love in my heart was joined by another throb lower down. He'd rolled up his shirtsleeves to reveal the inked forearms I'd fixated on more than once.

I stifled the little well of guilt at my white lie when I murmured, 'You are…you big lug.'

He reached me and lifted me easily off the lounger, despite my massive belly.

'Vito!' I gasped as I grabbed him around the neck.

'Who is calling who big, *bella*?' His husky chuckle had the throb going ballistic as his lips nuzzled my ear.

'Jesus, you two, get a room!' Évie laughed, apparently already over her misguided crush on Vito's brother as she slipped on a warm robe to cover herself too.

Dante would be dealt with eventually, and hopefully Evie would never need to know about the more dangerous or brutal aspects of the life I'd chosen, I'd decided.

Vito turned and began to carry me back across the terrace towards the steps leading to our suite.

'Where are you taking me, Vito?'

'I am doing what your sister suggests and taking you to my bed. It is too cold to use the pool today,' he said, clearly as unimpressed as his staff that Evie and I had wanted to take advatage of the first sign of sun in over a month. 'And I have been without you for days…' he declared, the demand in his voice making me melt in all the right places.

'But I was talking to my sister,' I protested, not very convincingly thanks to the breathless yearning already making my nipples pebble and my thighs quiver.

'Your sister will have to wait. Now you must please your man,' he said, going the full bossy as he stalked up the stairs with me in his arms.

When we arrived at the suite, he kicked the door closed behind him and dropped me on my feet. After pulling off my warm rode, he tugged his shirt over his head, buttons popping onto the floor. I edged back towards the bed as he proceeded to kick off his shoes and undo his fly. How much he needed me was evident from the huge bulge in his boxers and the dark demand on his face when he shoved them down.

'On the bed, Mia, now!' he growled as he stalked towards me. 'I have waited long enough.'

I backed up, forced to sit on the bed, then waddle back as he climbed up onto it too, to cage me in.

I lay back, my bikini doing nothing to disguise my need. He plucked at the strings, and within seconds I was naked, the yearning becoming turbo-charged.

'Who made you the boss of me?' I whispered, recalling the arguments we'd once had as I pressed my palm to his stubbled cheek and let my affection for him show.

He clasped my hand and dragged it away from his face to wrap it around his huge erection.

'You did, Mia,' he murmured, then leaned down and kissed me, thrusting his tongue deep in the dance of dominance and submission I adored. As he explored my slick folds with knowing fingers, brushing my needy clit and making me ride his hand while I stroked him, he whispered, 'As you are the boss of me, too.'

The rush of love was as overpowering as the rush of endorphins scenting the air while I climaxed.

He flipped me over, drawing me onto my knees so he could thrust himself deep while I was still clenching, spiraling upwards. He rode me to that glorious oblivion again and again as he cupped my breasts, stroked my belly and gave us both what we needed.

Hours later, after we'd showered and dined with Evie on our suite's private terrace, he took me to bed again. And as we lay together, exhausted, his hard chest pressed against my back, his hands stroking the mound of my pregnancy, the baby kicked.

'*Il bambino* is restless tonight,' he murmured against my hair.

'I think maybe you woke him up, Mr Insatiable,' I announced, loving his deep chuckle of response.

'I think maybe he is concerned that his mother is not fully mine yet...'

It took me a moment to make sense of the rumbled words through the endorphin haze, but when the meaning of them registered, I heard the regret in his tone, as well as the demand.

I shifted around so I could see Vito's face in the moonlight coming through the terrace doors. 'What do you mean, Vito? You know I'm yours, always.'

He clasped my cheek to brush my sweaty hair back from my face.

'We must be married, Mia, for you to truly be mine always.'

I stared at him, not sure what to say.

It wasn't the first time he'd demanded I marry him. But I'd put him off, not because I wasn't sure about him or about my love for him, but because I knew we both had a lot on our plates at the moment. He was still figuring out how to deal with Dante and end the blood feud his father had started so long ago, and I was concentrating on the birth of our baby. A wedding on top of that seemed like too much.

'Vito, I...'

He pressed his finger to my lips. 'Do not tell me no again, Mia.'

I shook off his finger, not liking that dictatorial tone

of voice. 'I didn't tell you no. I just said we should wait until…'

'If this is about a wedding,' he interrupted me, 'that can wait until you are ready, but I want to declare you as my wife, Mia. In front of man and God, before the baby arrives, and we are running out of time.' His hand slid down to my belly to stroke the distended flesh, his thumb cruising along the line which had appeared bisecting my belly button. 'I brought a priest with me from Rome for us to exchange our vows tomorrow night.'

I sat up in bed, frowning, the prickle of irritation growing that he wasn't giving me a choice, that he was pressuring me. 'So, are you *asking* me to marry you, or *telling* me, Vito?' I demanded.

He sat up too, but instead of meeting my anger with anger of his own, he clasped my neck to drag me to him. He covered my mouth with his, stifling any more protests. The kiss was deep, demanding, forceful, and as possessive as always, but when he dragged his lips away, leaving us both panting, both aching, he pressed his forehead to mine and rested his hand on my belly.

'If you are truly mine, Mia, why is this wrong?'

The gently asked question and the confusion on his face were my undoing. And all my objections dissolved in a rush of pure, unadulterated love.

Tears scalded my eyes. And my bottom lip began to quiver. 'I guess…it isn't,' I managed, conceding defeat, even as joy wrapped around my heart. 'I want to be yours, always. Let's make it official.'

'*Brava ragazza*,' he murmured, a sensual smile making my heart pulse hard in my chest. He kissed me again, licking the tears off my cheeks, then wrapped his arms around me to lift me against his broad chest and hold me tight.

The next evening, we were married in front of Evie and Lorenzo and several of his other men, while the household staff arranged a feast for everyone.

I said my vows in my faltering Italian, and then the priest—who I suspected Vito had probably strong-armed from Rome—blessed us both.

Later that night, Vito sealed our union by taking me in slow, sensual waves, rocking into my body again and again, filling my heart and soul to bursting as he brought us both to a shattering orgasm.

I was a mafia don's wife, and I couldn't have been happier.

Vito

Three hours later

The sound of banging had me waking up too fast, shattering the blissful dreams of Mia, my wife.

'Shhh…' I heard her stir beside me.

I threw off the bed sheet and stalked through the suite, ready to eviscerate whoever the hell it was hammering on the door. But when I tugged it open, Lorenzo stood there with a machine gun in his hands, his eyes wild.

'What the hell is going on that you would disturb our wedding night?' I demanded.

'It is Dante, *padrone*,' Lorenzo said, his voice shaking with anger.

Dante? What the fuck?

'Tell me!' I demanded.

'He escaped, during the wedding we think. We do not

know how. He tied up the men guarding him and then waited.'

'Dante is loose on the island?' Fury blindsided me, especially when I heard Mia's shocked whisper from behind me.

'D-Dante's escaped?'

I turned to see her standing in the moonlight with a thin wrap covering her nakedness.

'He stole a boat and got away ten minutes ago,' Lorenzo said. 'We fired on him, but then we had to let him go…'

I grabbed a shirt from the dresser, the fury making my head feel as if it was about to explode. 'Why the fuck did you let him escape?' I said, tugging on the clothing, then reaching for my gun.

'Because he had Signora Rocco's sister tied to him.'

'He's kidnapped Evie!' Mia's cry had me swinging round. I lurched forward, catching her before she could crumple to the floor.

I scooped her into my arms.

'Vito, you have to get her back!' she cried, the distress in her eyes tearing my heart out. 'I should have let you kill him when you had the chance…' she said, the fear in her voice crucifying me.

'Do not worry. We will get her back. He will not hurt her,' I said, determined to believe it. I could not be sure what that bastard would do to her. But Dante was an intelligent man, shrewd and smart as well as wild. Even if he had kidnapped her simply to make good his escape and use her as a shield against my men's bullets, he would surely also know that hurting her would be signing his own death warrant. And a part of me could not believe even now, that a boy who had once defended his mother so zealously would deliberately hurt a defenseless woman.

But when Mia spasmed in my arms, and I heard the deep moan of pain and felt the gush of water against my pantleg, Dante and Evie's fate was propelled to the back of my mind.

'Vito!' Mia cried, gripping my shirt. 'I think… I think the baby's coming…'

'Lorenzo, get the doctor out of bed.' I threw the demand over my shoulder, making a promise to myself that if anything happened to Mia or my child tonight, Dante would not live to see morning.

Mia

Four hours later

I lay shaking, sore and exhausted, my arms so tired I could barely lift them, as Vito cradled me and our baby against his chest and kissed our son's damp head.

'He is beautiful, Mia, just as you are,' he whispered.

I looked up at my husband, tears stinging my eyes. The birth had been much swifter than expected, and predictably excruciating, with Vito threatening the poor doctor and his nurses with all sorts of retribution if they did not take my pain away, until I'd finally managed to convince him to let them do their jobs.

I stared at our son, his tiny fists clasped tight, his face screwed up in protest, before he let out another series of tired wails. I pressed my nipple to his mouth, and he latched on greedily.

He was three weeks early, but according to the obstetrician Vito had hired weeks ago, our son was healthy and more than large enough to survive without an incubator.

His lungs were certainly in good working order.

'Wh-what's happening with the search for Dante and Evie?' I asked.

I'd managed to push the terrifying thoughts about my sister's safety to the back of my mind while I had concentrated on bringing our baby into the world, but now he was safe and well—and beautiful, I thought, blinking back more tears—the fear returned.

Vito brushed my hair back from my face and placed a kiss on my forehead. 'Do not worry, Mia. I am confident we will get her back unharmed. I promise you, he will not hurt her.'

'How do you know that?' I asked.

'He is a bad man, a wild man, a dangerous man, but not one who would hurt a woman, I think. And she is… how do you say…his trump card. He has already sent a text on her phone, saying he wishes to negotiate a truce for Evie's safe return.'

'He… He has?' I asked, hope surging. 'But if he's willing to negotiate now, why didn't he do that before?'

'Because he was a prisoner here. He wished to bargain from a position of strength. Taking your sister, escaping from here was part of his plan. This is why he has refused to sanction any deal for so long, I think.'

I nodded. Trying not to let my fear swamp me.

All I could do was hope now that Vito was right. And Dante wouldn't hurt Evie.

I stared down at my baby…at our baby…clamped tight on my nipple, sucking voraciously. I smiled a watery smile. I trusted his daddy, implicitly. Not just to rescue Evie, but also to be honest with me about the threat Dante represented.

'All we must do now is wait for him to decide what it is he wants. Then the negotiations begin.' Vito said, pressing his large hand to our baby's head. 'And you, Signora Rocco,' he said, his voice heavy with pride, 'your job is to rest and recover after giving me the most beautiful son in the world.'

I yawned, so totally drained, emotionally as well as physically, it felt impossibly good to have Vito's muscular arms around us both.

'For once, I think I might do what you tell me to without an argument,' I murmured, and he let out a husky laugh of approval.

Capturing my chin between his thumb and forefinger, he lifted my mouth for his kiss. *'Brava ragazza.'*

I felt the love flow between us as his lips covered mine. I swallowed down the lump of panic lodged in my throat as exhaustion overwhelmed me.

Tomorrow we would concentrate on getting Evie back and ending this bloody feud once and for all, but tonight was for us. And our baby boy. And our love. Which was the bedrock of this family now.

Hopefully one day soon, Dante would realise that, too.

* * * * *

If you couldn't put down Italian Devil's Baby,
then be sure to check out Dante *and* Evie's *story—*
the next instalment in the
Captive Mafia Seductions *duet, coming soon!*
And why not try these other stories
from Heidi Rice?

Princess for the Headlines
Billionaire's Wedlocked Wife
The Heir Affair
Greek's Kidnapped Princess
Boss's Bride Price

Available now!